"Calchas and Phobos are waiting for me," Lucian said. "If I don't go to their chambers, they'll come looking for me. If I try to hide, they'll turn the palace upside down until they find me. I have to get out. What else can I do?"

Menyas chewed his lips and thought for a moment. "I don't see anything better. Yes, lad, I'm afraid you'll have to clear out. Fast and far. Before those two get their hooks into you. All right, you stay quiet and wait here. I'll collect a few things you'll need."

Menyas hurried into the stables. Lucian sat down and put his head in his hands. One of the donkeys nuzzled him. He glanced up. The animal was scruffy, with patches of hair missing from his back and haunches; his ribs stood out, his long ears were notched and ragged; all in all, the most wretched-looking jackass that Lucian had ever seen.

"You're a sorry sight, poor beast," Lucian murmured, "but you've less to worry about than I do."

"I doubt it," said the jackass.

"A rousing adventure complete with cliffhangers and do-or-die situations."   —*School Library Journal,* starred review

"Part Greek myth, part *Canterbury Tales,* part *Wizard of Oz.* . . . Done in epic style, the book almost brims over with tales, twists, and trouble."   —*Booklist*

The ARKADIANS

The King's Fountain
The Marvelous Misadventures of Sebastian
The Truthful Harp
Coll and His White Pig
Time Cat
The Flagship Hope: Aaron Lopez
Border Hawk: August Bondi
My Five Tigers

Books for Adults
Fifty Years in the Doghouse
Park Avenue Vet (with Dr. Louis J. Camuti)
My Love Affair with Music
Janine Is French
And Let the Credit Go

Translations
Nausea, by Jean-Paul Sartre
The Wall, by Jean-Paul Sartre
The Sea Rose, by Paul Vialar
Uninterrupted Poetry, by Paul Eluard

The ARKADIANS
Lloyd Alexander

PUFFIN BOOKS

PUFFIN BOOKS
Published by the Penguin Group
Penguin Books USA Inc., 375 Hudson Street, New York, New York 10014, U.S.A.
Penguin Books Ltd, 27 Wrights Lane, London W8 5TZ, England
Penguin Books Australia Ltd, Ringwood, Victoria, Australia
Penguin Books Canada Ltd, 10 Alcorn Avenue, Toronto, Ontario, Canada M4V 3B2
Penguin Books (N.Z.) Ltd, 182-190 Wairau Road, Auckland 10, New Zealand

Penguin Books Ltd, Registered Offices: Harmondsworth, Middlesex, England

First published in the United States of America by Dutton Children's Books,
a division of Penguin USA Inc., 1995
Published in Puffin Books, 1997

1 3 5 7 9 10 8 6 4 2

THE LIBRARY OF CONGRESS HAS CATALOGED THE DUTTON EDITION AS FOLLOWS:
Alexander, Lloyd
The Arkadians / by Lloyd Alexander—st ed.
p. cm.
Summary: To escape the wrath of the king and his wicked soothsayers,
an honest young man joins with a poet-turned-jackass and a young girl
with mystical powers on a series of epic adventures.
ISBN 0-525-45415-2
[1. Fantasy.] I. Title.
PZ7.A3774Ar 1995
[Fic]—dc20 94-35025
CIP AC

Puffin Books ISBN 0-14-038073-6
Printed in the United States of America

For hopeful storytellers
and fond listeners

Contents

Contents

The ARKADIANS

MT. PANTHEA

Sanctuary of the
Lady of Wild Things

Land of
the Horse Clan

Village of the Goat Folk

N

MT. LERNA

Cave of
Woman-Who-
Talks-to-Snakes

METARA

TAUROS

NAXOS

ARKADIA

CALLISTA

Map by Claudia Carlson

I

King Bromios and
Woman-Who-Talks-to-Snakes

This is the tale of a jackass and a young bean counter, a girl of marvels and mysteries, horsemen swift as wind, Goat Folk, Daughters of Morning, voyages, tempests, terrors, disasters. And the occasional rainbow.

But all this is yet to come, and our tale begins with King Bromios and Woman-Who-Talks-to-Snakes.

So: When Bromios was chosen king of Arkadia, long custom obliged him to seek a prophecy from the oracle pythoness, Woman-Who-Talks-to-Snakes, in her cave at Mount Lerna. Bromios, for his part, would have gladly avoided the whole squirmy business. He was a heavy-fisted, barrel-chested man with a big voice and a hard head; no coward, certainly, but any thought of snakes made his flesh creep.

His royal soothsayers, Calchas and Phobos, insisted.

"Allow me to remind Your Majesty," said Calchas, "when our Bear tribe forefathers came to Arkadia, they found a shocking state of affairs: a country governed by councils of women, all devoted to that figment of female imagination, the Lady of Wild Things. Knowing it only proper for men to command and women to obey—a simple truth that women seem incapable of grasping— our heroic warriors overthrew the councils and made themselves lords of the land. Since then, your subjects have enjoyed the rule of kings—guided, naturally, by the unerring advice of their soothsayers."

"The women, however, cling foolishly to their old ways," added Phobos. "They still believe in the Lady of Wild Things; and the pythoness is venerated as highly as the Lady herself."

"Seeking your prophecy is a mere formality," said Calchas, waving a plump, bejeweled hand, "observed only because the women expect it. Otherwise, they would be most unsettled."

"They're women," said Bromios, "so what does it matter?"

"An alarming number of men also revere the Lady." Phobos pressed his thin lips and shook his head. "Which is absurd, since she does not exist. Has any of us ever seen her? Received the slightest sign from her? Of course not."

"What better proof?" said Calchas. "If she existed, I and my dear colleague would, surely, be the first to know."

Calchas and Phobos were authorities in such matters. They were skilled at finding signs and portents in stars, clouds, flights of birds, and chicken gizzards. On the death of the old king, the pair consulted one of the oracular chickens, nicely roasted, understood that Bromios was to be monarch, and so proclaimed him.

"As for the Lady's followers," Calchas went on, "their devotion to her lessens their devotion to Your Majesty. They should be encouraged—vigorously encouraged—to see the error of their ways. This, I foretell, will happen when the time is ripe. At the moment, it would be imprudent to rub them the wrong way."

"Your Majesty must visit the pythoness," said Phobos. "A question of state policy."

"Policy, policy, whatever that is," grumbled Bromios. As the old king's war leader, he preferred yelling and smacking heads to sitting on a throne. More comfortable using his fists instead of his brains, he had been tempted to decline the honor. Calchas and Phobos promised that he would seldom, if ever, have to think at all. Few kings did. It was not required.

"I won't have to touch any snakes?" said Bromios.

"No, no, no." Calchas brushed aside the notion.

"Nothing like that. You go, you listen to some nonsensical babbling, and you come back. Goodwill all around, and everyone satisfied."

"You're sure about the snakes?" said Bromios.

Next morning, Bromios rode the half-day's journey from his palace in Metara to Mount Lerna, his bodyguard galloping with him, Calchas and Phobos carried in litters at the rear. As the soothsayers advised, Bromios wore full regalia: the bearskin cloak, the necklace of bear teeth and claws, the bear's head helmet. His leather leggings were bound with thongs, his thick-soled boots made him look even taller than he was. At his side hung the great two-handed sword. Bromios himself had cheered up and felt royally scornful of any stupid old hag of a snake-woman.

When the road ended, he had to climb off his horse and go tramping down an overgrown, winding path. Calchas and Phobos, on either side, guided him deeper into the woods. The weather had turned mild, though streaks of snow still whitened the upper slopes of Mount Lerna. The Sky Bear had rolled the sun high into the cloudless blue, golden shafts of light bathed the clearing and danced over the pool at the mountain's foot. Even so, Bromios suddenly shivered. He had the nasty impression that many beady little eyes watched him from the bushes.

Near the edge of the pool stood a ring of stone col-umns and broken archways. Taking his arms, Calchas and Phobos led him past these old ruins to a tumble of huge boulders. The entry to the cave was a narrow, jag-ged cleft in the rock. What with his heavy cloak, he could barely squeeze through. No sooner had he stepped inside than flames sprang up and ghostly white shapes floated toward him.

He stumbled back, flung one hand to his eyes, the other to his sword hilt. Then he blew out his breath in relief. The ghosts were two small girls wearing white tu-nics and holding torches. The chamber in which he found himself was large, reaching some distance into the shadows.

"Bromios?" A high, clear voice echoed all around him.

Bromios answered with an angry growl. A king should not be startled like that.

Calchas spoke up. "Yes. Here is the Bear King, Lord of Arkadia. He will see the pythoness."

A third, taller girl dressed in a blue robe had ap-peared as if from nowhere. In each hand, she carried a clay cup. With a graceful gesture, she offered one of the vessels to Bromios.

"Drink, O Bear King. This is the Water of Forgetting."

Bromios shifted uneasily and scowled at Calchas. "You didn't tell me about this part," he muttered. "What's the brew? Poison, for all I know."

"To cleanse your mind of all concerns for the world outside," said the girl. "Think only of this moment, here and now."

"Drink it, drink it," whispered Calchas. "It's plain water."

"Not thirsty," snapped Bromios.

"Drink it anyway," said Phobos. "Let them get on with their rigmarole."

Bromios made a face and gulped down the contents. He licked his teeth. Water it was, and icy.

The girl handed him the other cup. "The Water of Remembering, so that you may forever recall what you will see and hear."

Bromios swallowed hastily and wiped his mouth on the back of his hand. The two little girls raised their torches and beckoned him to follow. With Calchas and Phobos nudging him from behind, Bromios trod warily to the rear of the cave, where stone steps led downward. The girls descended easily and lightly, but Bromios nearly lost his footing on the stones worn smooth and slippery. He must have drunk the water too quickly, for his head pounded and his stomach gurgled. He clenched his jaw to keep his teeth from chattering. Even under the heavy fur cloak, Bromios felt so cold, so cold.

The steps ended on the earthen floor of a long, domed chamber. Flames from iron braziers made the walls seem awash in blood. A sickly sweet smell of incense choked his nostrils and made his eyes water. He stopped in his tracks. No one had told him to, he simply did. A dozen paces ahead was a deep recess hewn into the living rock. Hunched on a high, three-legged stool sat the pythoness.

Moldering black robes shrouded the frail, stoop-shouldered figure; covering her face was a mask of polished silver crowned with a tangle of silver serpents. In the shadows behind her, Bromios thought he glimpsed the rolling coils of some horrid reptile.

The pythoness straightened and shook her head, as if rousing from a long dream. The gleaming mask turned full upon Bromios: a woman's features, a calm expression frozen in the metal. When at last she spoke, the voice rang hollow.

"Bear King, do you truly desire your prophecy?"

"That's why I'm here, isn't it?" grumbled Bromios, adding under his breath, "Why else would I come into this foul den?"

"So be it, then." The pythoness paused. When she spoke again, her tone was thin and faint, the words seeming to come from some great distance:

"O Bromios, Bromios,
Your life-threads are spun.
A city in ashes, a king in rags,
And then your course is run."

The pythoness bowed her head and folded her arms. Bromios waited, but she remained silent.

"Let's have the rest of it," Bromios demanded impatiently.

"There is nothing more."

"What?" cried Bromios. "That's all? Ashes? Rags?"

"As you heard."

Bromios was no quick thinker, but it took hardly any time for him to grasp that he had been given something unpleasant.

"Take it back," he ordered. "Give me a better one."

"I cannot do so."

"You will!" shouted Bromios. "Don't tell me ashes and rags. I won't stomach that."

"I fear you must."

"Change it!" roared Bromios. "Right now! Do as I command, you scruffy old hag." He stepped forward, hand on sword.

"Silence!" The pythoness slid from her perch to stand straight and tall. She pointed at Bromios. "No closer. I am Woman-Who-Talks-to-Snakes!"

Bromios felt his words shrivel in his throat and his fingers freeze on the hilt. With all his might, he tried to draw the weapon. In vain.

"Take your prophecy and leave." The voice of the pythoness filled the grotto and thundered in the king's ears. Her eyes blazed through the slits in the mask. The crown of serpents seemed to writhe and hiss. "Go. Before I lose my temper and set the snakes on you."

Bromios had been standing with one foot rooted to the ground, the other poised in midstride. Now he spun around and plunged headlong up the steps, Calchas and Phobos scrambling behind. He burst from the cave, went crashing through the undergrowth as if a dozen serpents were at his heels, and galloped for Metara as fast as his horse's legs could carry him.

Safe inside his palace, behind the bolted doors of his inner chambers, Bromios vented his wrath. He roared, ground his teeth, shook his fists, kicked over tables, smashed bowls and goblets, all the while cursing and threatening Woman-Who-Talks-to-Snakes.

"If I could get my hands around her skinny neck!" he shouted. "I want her rooted out! Put down, cut off, done away with!"

While Bromios ranted on, Calchas and Phobos exchanged glances.

"I wonder," Calchas murmured, raising an eyebrow,

"if this might indeed be the moment? Has the time turned ripe sooner than we hoped?"

"To end the pernicious influence of the Lady of Wild Things?" said Phobos. "Yes, dear colleague, I believe the perfect opportunity has just been presented to us."

With the enthusiastic approval of his soothsayers, Bromios sent warriors to Mount Lerna. They filled the pool to the brim with dirt and gravel, stopped up the spring that fed it, and toppled the circle of columns. The cave was empty. They piled boulders to block the entrance.

They could not find the pythoness. Woman-Who-Talks-to-Snakes and her maidens had vanished as completely as if they had never been there. The only trace of her, which the warriors carried back to Bromios, was the silver mask.

It appeared to be smiling.

2

Lucian and the Jackass

During the weeks that followed, Bromios turned more gloomy than wrathful. Worn out by roaring curses and breaking furniture, he spent most of the days chewing his nails and pacing his chambers, demanding to know why his warriors, presently scouring the countryside, had not yet laid hold of Woman-Who-Talks-to-Snakes.

Also he sent heralds to towns and villages, proclaiming it forbidden under pain of death to observe practices or customs having anything to do with the Lady of Wild Things: a heavy blow to wise-women, healers, midwives, water-finders, and such, for they were all followers of the Lady. This was declared in the king's name but actually was done at the urging of Calchas and Phobos, who commended Bromios for his wisdom and strength of character.

"That," Calchas remarked confidentially to Phobos, "should put these women in their place and keep them in it once and for all. High time, too."

"Indeed so, dear colleague," replied Phobos. "Further, since we are the ones who decide what is lawful and what is not, in practical terms we have as much power as Bromios himself."

"And considerably greater opportunities," said Calchas. "On the whole, things have fallen out more profitably than we could have foretold."

Meantime, while Bromios gloomed and glowered and the soothsayers congratulated each other, a clerk named Lucian went about his duties in the royal counting house.

Now, this Lucian was a large-framed, long-legged young man, mostly knees and elbows, and more by way of ear size than he really needed. His mother had been a palace cook; his father, a harness maker. Orphaned in earliest childhood, he had grown up in the kitchens and stables. Sturdy enough to be a palace guard, he was judged too nimble-witted for a military future. He could read and write, was quick at numbers, and showed so much promise that he had risen from sweeper to pot scraper; later, to archive copier. This very week, when the post fell suddenly vacant, he had been put in charge of inventories and accounts.

Lucian told himself he should be grateful; all the more since he had no prospect for any different occupation. If he applied himself, worked hard, did as he was told, and kept out of trouble, he could look forward to a long life doing exactly what he was doing. Which he hated, when he stopped to think about it; and so he thought about it rarely. He loved hearing every kind of tale or story, but that was the only serious flaw in his character.

Late on this particular afternoon, Lucian was in his cubbyhole, rummaging through boxes of scrolls and records of past accounts. At that moment, Calchas himself happened to pass by. He cast a cold fish eye on Lucian and the jumble of documents and demanded to know the reason for such disorder.

"Lord Calchas," Lucian said, getting to his feet, "my accounts don't balance. Something's wrong, but if I've made a mistake I can't find it."

"Mistake?" snapped Calchas. "It does not please me to hear of mistakes. They signify slackness and weak moral fiber, which I do not tolerate."

"But my sums are correct, as you can see." Lucian held out a slate covered with figures. "Only they don't tally with the provisions in the storehouse."

"Indeed?" Calchas had been about to turn away but now he stepped closer to Lucian. "Exactly how did you arrive at that conclusion?"

"My Lord, I've gone myself and counted every bean, every drop of oil, everything. I don't find what's supposed to be there. But it's been recorded as bought, and a great deal of money paid out.

"So much goods can't disappear into thin air," Lucian pressed on. "Rats couldn't have eaten them all. Were they stolen? Or even bought in the first place? Lord Phobos and your honorable self authorized the purchases, but I can't find who got the money—"

Lucian choked off his words. The soothsayer's pink cheeks had gone dead white, glistening with little beads of sweat, and his mouth seemed to be chewing on air. Lucian's blood froze as he suddenly understood that the answer to who got the money was standing in front of him. The realization took his breath away. He dared say no more. He felt as if a very large pit had opened at his feet and he had nearly blundered over the edge.

Calchas regained his composure and smiled. "What a painstaking young man you are. Now, my good fellow, tell me what you propose doing about it."

"I—I don't know. First, I thought I'd take it up with the chief steward, but—"

"That would be quite proper," Calchas said smoothly. "Only consider: Would it be prudent? The chief steward might see this business in a different and unfavorable light, reflecting your own incompetence. You yourself could be blamed, with painful consequences.

"No, you will not report this mysterious state of affairs. Lord Phobos and I shall do it for you. We can explain your difficulties more lucidly and sympathetically. With you, there might be some doubt as to your honesty. Whereas, our veracity is beyond question."

Lucian did not answer. Calchas, beaming, clamped a hand on Lucian's shoulder.

"Our pleasant little conversation has proved most fortunate," remarked the soothsayer. "It has made me realize that you are far too intelligent and enterprising to waste your talents counting beans and scribbling numbers.

"It just so happens that Lord Phobos and I require an assistant, a young apprentice to learn our sacrificial procedures. The question: Where to find a suitable individual? The answer: Here he stands. Namely, yourself. Yes, my dear young man, the very position for you."

Lucian bowed his head; not out of respectful gratitude but to keep the soothsayer from reading the expression on his face. He could imagine all too clearly the sacrificial procedures Calchas had in mind.

"Come to our chambers," ordered the soothsayer, giving Lucian an affectionate tug on the ear. "By sundown, no later. Ah—yes, I shall take those obviously erroneous documents with me."

At that, Calchas snatched the papers, gathered up his robes, and went down the passageway as fast as he could waddle. The instant the soothsayer was out of sight, Lucian took to his heels in the opposite direction, running to find his closest friend in the palace, Menyas, the old stableman.

He was in a cold sweat when he reached the yard in front of the storehouses. There, one of the royal provisioners, a rough-bearded merchant called Cerdo, had just arrived and was bustling about, shouting at porters to haul away sacks and baskets of goods. Menyas was tethering Cerdo's pack animals to a railing. Lucian pressed through the huddle of mules and donkeys.

"Menyas, listen to me." He seized the stableman's arm. "I'm in trouble. I have to get away from them. They're going to kill me—" He blurted out a hasty account of his encounter with Calchas.

"Whoa, there, whoa." Menyas shook his grizzled head. "Let me get a saddle on this business. Goods missing, money paid, nothing to show for it? Eh, there's a mucky smell to all that. As for you being done away with—I wouldn't put anything past those royal chicken pluckers. They won't be skittish about cutting your throat to save their necks. If you're sure that's what they mean to do—"

"You should have seen the look on Calchas's face. He knows I'm onto the scheme. He and Phobos are waiting for me. If I don't go to their chambers, they'll come looking for me. If I try to hide, they'll turn the palace upside down until they find me. I have to get out. What else can I do?"

Menyas chewed his lips and thought for a moment. "I don't see anything better. Yes, lad, I'm afraid you'll have to clear out. Fast and far. Before those two get their hooks into you. All right, you stay quiet and wait here. I'll collect a few things you'll need."

Menyas hurried into the stables. Lucian sat down and put his head in his hands. One of the donkeys nuzzled him. He glanced up. The animal was scruffy, with patches of hair missing from his back and haunches; his ribs stood out, his long ears were notched and ragged; all in all, the most wretched-looking jackass that Lucian had ever seen.

"You're a sorry sight, poor beast," Lucian murmured, "but you've less to worry about than I do."

"I doubt it," said the jackass. "I overheard your plans for an immediate departure. A wise decision. Furthermore, I beg you in the name of mercy: Set me free of this terrible merchant, Cerdo. Take me with you."

3

Unfortunate Fronto

I'm sorry," Lucian began. "I don't think I could—" He stopped short. "What am I doing? Talking to a jackass! And he's talking to me?"

"Indeed, I am," said the jackass. "I believe I expressed myself in the clearest possible terms, but let me try again. My dear young man, I need help. Require assistance. Implore your aid. Now, if I have your full attention—"

Lucian stared. Head spinning, he tried to scrape together as much sanity as he could. Common sense told him he was not holding a conversation with a donkey. The voice, he decided, came from someone crouching among the pack animals. He bent down to find whoever was hiding. He saw no one.

"You? You spoke?" Lucian stammered. "How? You can't. You're a jackass."

"My name is Fronto," the beast replied in a tone of wounded dignity. "I'm not a jackass. I'm a poet, though some might call that one and the same."

"I'm dreaming this," Lucian murmured. "Or lost my wits. Whatever, something's gone wrong with me."

"Gone wrong with *me* would more accurately describe the situation," said Fronto. "Horrible, monstrous. Never mind the details, I'll discuss them later. Right now, all I want is to be out of Cerdo's clutches. A matter of life and death. Mine. If you call it a life in this humiliating carapace, this asinine shell."

"Shell?" said Lucian, relieved by this peculiar but at least plausible explanation. "Someone stitched you into a donkey skin? Here, I'll peel it off."

He began tugging at Fronto's ears and mane, trying to strip away the shaggy hide.

"Stop, stop!" Fronto tossed his head and reared on his hind legs. "This is all me. I've been transformed, transmogrified. I'm jackass through and through."

"That's—terrible," said Lucian, at a loss for a better way to put it. Though still bewildered, he was growing a little more used to the idea of a talking jackass. "Uncomfortable, too."

"Understatement," said Fronto. "*Litotes*, to use the rhetorical term. Now that you seem to have grasped my predicament, I entreat you to do something about it. And about your own, as well.

"And you're quite right," Fronto added. "Those larcenous soothsayers, those sanctimonious frauds, are stealing money hand over fist. And I'll tell you something else: Cerdo's in the scheme with them. He gets a fat share to line his own purse. I know. I heard him bragging to his cronies. They're all as crooked as a ram's horns, and murderous into the bargain. Unless you get moving as fast as you can, you won't live out this day. Unless I get free of that brute, I won't last much longer."

"Menyas can help you better than I can," said Lucian. "He's good with horses—donkeys, too, I'm sure. You'll explain to him—"

"No." Fronto stamped his hooves. "When I see the effect my deplorable state had on you, no telling what it may do to him. Least said, soonest mended—as I wrote in one of my more successful odes. Unlike poets, most people get upset over apparent impossibility. The question is: Will you take me along? Since you're departing anyway—"

Fronto broke off. Menyas was there, with a bundle on his shoulder.

"Best I could do at short notice, but it should tide you over a while. A little money, too," he added, slipping coins into Lucian's hand. "Quick, now. Out the back gate. The guard's not on duty yet."

As the stableman began hustling Lucian from the yard, Fronto flicked his tail and made sounds of clearing his throat. Lucian held back. "One thing more. This jackass. I want him."

"Steal one of Cerdo's pack animals? For a bean counter, you're turning into a bold rogue. Well, why not? You're in such trouble now, a little extra won't matter. But snaffle a good mount, at least. Don't bother with this miserable beast."

"Him," said Lucian. "No other."

"He's a rawboned wreck, two steps from the boneyard. For heaven's sake, lad, why?"

"He asked me—I mean, look at him. He wants to go with me as clearly as if he spoke the words."

"All right, all right, whatever you say. We can't lose time wrangling over this piece of crow bait." Menyas hoisted the bundle and roped it onto Fronto's back. "There. Let him make himself useful, anyway."

That moment, Cerdo came out of the grain shed. Seeing Lucian and Fronto hurrying from the yard, he began bawling at the top of his voice: "Thief! Donkey robber!"

"Giddyap," cried Menyas, giving Lucian a shove and Fronto a smack to speed them on their way. "I'll deal with him."

Leaving the stableman doing all he could to hinder the furious merchant, Lucian darted through the alley behind the storehouse, Fronto after him, and clattered along the wooden walkways, past the fenced-in run for the oracular chickens. Like most of the palace, the back gate was made of timber; it was so seldom used, however, that the bolt had frozen in its socket. Lucian, despite his efforts, could not draw it free. He flung himself against it, hammering with his fists, battering with his shoulders.

"Allow me," said Fronto. He turned and kicked out with his hind legs. The door sagged; and as the assault continued, it broke loose and fell open.

Fronto plunged out. Lucian, having not the slightest idea where they were going, could only seize the poet's tail and let himself be pulled along. Only after they had crossed the public square did Fronto slow his pace. He trotted briskly down winding lanes, through back alleys, clambering over rubbish heaps, and nipping around corners. Lucian, who had never set foot beyond the palace walls, asked how he knew his way in such a maze.

"I've had some previous experience," said Fronto, "eluding tiresome creditors, tavern keepers, magistrates, not to mention physically aggressive critics. For poets, that's an essential skill, an art as necessary as turning a rhyme. Sometimes more so."

No sooner had Fronto finished speaking than Lucian cried out. He was spun around and a lantern thrust up to his face.

"Here, now, let's have a look at you." A city watchman was peering at him. "What are you up to, eh?"

"Ah—sir, we—that is, I—" Lucian choked, then went on quickly. "Yes, glad I found you. At the palace —a terrible commotion. The oracular chickens got loose. They're flapping all over the streets. I was ordered to summon every watchman to go after them."

"Then, fool, don't waste time yammering." The man set off with all haste toward the palace.

"You have a glib tongue," said Fronto as they hurried on. "A nice bit of invention, those chickens."

"I had to think of something. I couldn't let him arrest us." Lucian grinned with wry satisfaction. "I never had to tell a lie before."

"It gets easier with practice," said Fronto.

They reached the outskirts of Metara without further challenge, but it was well after nightfall by the time they passed the outlying farms and made their way into the woodlands.

"Calchas and Phobos," Lucian said anxiously, "they'll be looking all over the place for me."

"Better to have them looking for you than finding you," said Fronto. "Don't worry. We're well away and safe here for the time being. I'd be much obliged if you'd remove this bundle your friend imposed on me."

As soon as Lucian did so, Fronto threw himself on the turf, rolling about and kicking his knobby legs in the air. Fearing the poet had gone into some kind of fit, Lucian started toward him.

"Sheer exuberance," Fronto assured him. "Animal spirits, literally and figuratively. At last free of Cerdo's clutches! What a relief, you can't imagine." After a few more rolls, the poet heaved himself upright. "I feel better already. This would be the crucial time—"

"To tell what happened to you," Lucian put in.

"—to explore the contents of that bundle. I suspect it holds edibles. I hope so, for my belly's empty as a drum."

Lucian hurried to untie the pack. Wrapped in a cloak were figs, cheese, some olives, a hunch of bread, and a large jar of wine. "I'm sorry. There's not much that you —a donkey, that is—would like."

"Not much?" cried Fronto. "A feast! One of the few advantages of my condition is that not only can I eat grass, thistles, hay, and all such disgusting vegetation, but human nourishment as well. My digestion is universally excellent. So, too, my appetite, growing keener with every fleeting moment."

Lucian spread out the provisions. Fronto munched away, bolting down his share, then helping Lucian to finish his own.

"That wine jar presents a small difficulty," said Fronto, chomping and belching at the same time. "Would you be kind enough to tip it into my mouth? On these occasions, hooves can be inconvenient."

He squatted on his haunches and stretched out his neck. Lucian held up the jar and poured some of the liquid down the poet's gullet. Fronto extended a long tongue and licked his lips.

"Pure nectar! I've had nothing like it since my regrettable accident."

"That's what I want to hear about," said Lucian.

"Just another taste," said Fronto. "It will clarify my mind. I've been treated like a donkey for such a while, sometimes I fear I've begun thinking like one."

Lucian did as requested, and with one gulp after the other, Fronto drained the jar. He nosed around to make sure nothing remained of the food, then settled back on his hindquarters.

"My dear Lucian, no human being is more miserable than a poet who has lost his inspiration. That was the situation in which I found myself a few weeks ago. My head was empty, my spirits leaden. What should have been winged words barely crept along, earthbound. The poetic spark had flickered out, the divine afflatus had blown away, creative rapture had fled; and my landlord, insensitive oaf, kept bringing up the question of rent. In short, a glorious career had come to an inglorious conclusion. What, I ask you, did I do?"

"I suppose," Lucian said, "you took up some other line of work."

"Abandon literature?" Fronto gave him a horrified look. "Impossible, unthinkable. Once a poet, always a poet. No, dear boy, I did what poets have always done in such a predicament. I flung myself to my knees and implored the Lady of Wild Things to send me inspiration."

"Fronto—" asked Lucian, shocked, "are you telling me you actually believe in—her?"

"Of course," replied Fronto. "All poets do. The Lady, as we well know, is the fountainhead of artistic intuition, eloquence, imagination. You don't suppose I'd direct my entreaties to some hairy, toothy ancestral bear. I was seeking inspiration, not hibernation.

"My continued supplications, alas, brought no result. My poetic spirit lay as lively as a dead mackerel. Then a thought came to me. I understood what must be done."

Here Fronto sighed and broke off. Lucian waited some long moments and finally asked, "What was it?"

Fronto did not reply. Rattling noises came from his open mouth. Lucian at first believed Fronto was sobbing, heartbroken by his own unhappy tale, until he realized the poet was snoring.

Impatient for the rest of the story, Lucian nudged him and prodded his flanks. Fronto stayed motionless, his long ears and shaggy head in stark outline against the moon. The poet had fallen unwakeably asleep.

Lucian, disappointed, could only curl up on the turf, pull the cloak over his shoulders, and try to do likewise.

4

Transformations

For a moment, on the ragged edge of wakefulness, Lucian believed a nightmare had ended, that he was on the straw pallet in his cubbyhole, his life was not in danger, and there had never been such a creature as a talking jackass. With a sigh of relief, he opened his eyes, blinked at the dawn light, and there he was, shivering on the turf, his cloak dew-drenched. With the truth of his situation like a cold lump in his stomach, he sat up and tried to rub away the chill in his bones and the crick in his neck.

Fronto was hunkered on the ground, still fast asleep. Lucian stepped over to him and prodded his flank, warning him it was daybreak.

"Really?" The poet opened one eye. "Yes, well, thank

you for that fascinating information. Wake me closer to noon, there's a good fellow."

Without Lucian's continued prodding, Fronto would have drowsed off. At last, with much yawning and head shaking, he got himself up on all four legs. "It's been some while since I've enjoyed a civilized morning's repose. With Cerdo, it was always the crack of the whip at the crack of dawn. In happier times—ah, how long ago they seem—I found it difficult to take anything seriously until midafternoon. However, if you insist. Did you mention breakfast?"

"The food's gone," said Lucian. "I should have put some aside."

"No matter," said Fronto. "Seize the day, whatever's in it to seize, before something comes along and seizes you. Had I known I'd end up a jackass, I'd have seized a lot more."

"Speaking of that," said Lucian, "you never told me what happened to you."

"I didn't?" said Fronto. "Ah—yes, you're right. I only meant to pause for dramatic effect, and here it's tomorrow already. Now, where was I?"

"You knew what you had to do."

"Exactly so." Fronto nodded and resumed his interrupted tale.

"At Mount Lerna, near the oracle's cave, there's a pool

dedicated to the Lady of Wild Things and strictly forbidden to men. It's said to have mysterious powers. The oracle, so I'd heard, drinks from it and receives her inspiration. I resolved to go to that pool—surely the Lady wouldn't begrudge me a few sips from it, all in a good cause.

"And so I did. Late one night, I stole into the grove. Not a soul in sight. I tiptoed to the edge of the pool, knelt, cupped a little water in my hands, drank it down, and waited eagerly for the glorious moment.

"Inspiration?" Fronto glumly went on. "Not a flicker. And yet, conditions should have been perfect: gnarled trees, whispering wind, moonshine so bright I could see my reflection in the limpid pool—the kind of atmosphere that's stock-in-trade for us poets. Had I been even halfway at the top of my bent, I'd have dashed off a dozen rhapsodies on the spot. But no, my only thought was I'd likely catch cold in such a damp and chilly spot.

"The difficulty was clear. I had not sufficiently imbibed the magical waters. I gulped down more and more. With no result. Did I say no result? Ah, my dear Lucian, there was a result, a most horrendous one. As I bent over the pool, I observed my reflection. Believe me, I make no claim to being in any way a handsome fellow—modesty has always been one of my endearing qualities—but I saw a blunt, hairy nose, certainly not mine, the end as white as if dipped in flour; ears long and shaggy. In short, the face of a jackass stared back at me.

"Aghast, I bent closer; so close I lost my balance and tumbled in headlong. I went floundering to the bottom, gasping for breath, suddenly so heavy I feared I'd never rise to the surface.

"But the pool was shallow and, at last, I managed to clamber out. On all fours! My hands and feet were hooves! My neck, elongated—and I had the distinct impression I had grown a tail. Terrified, I peered back into the pool. One glance confirmed it: I had become a complete ass."

"Horrible!" burst out Lucian, who had been hanging on Fronto's every word. "Enough to drive you mad!"

"Almost, but not quite," said Fronto. "We poets are used to finding ourselves in odd states, and I tried to keep my wits about me. I would go to the oracle, confess what I'd done, beg her forgiveness and help. She'd know how to deal with this kind of thing.

"I started toward the cave. That instant, a troop of palace warriors, brandishing swords and torches, came whooping into the glade. I bolted in panic. The last place in the world I wanted to be was in the midst of those rampaging ruffians.

"I galloped into the underbrush and hid until things quieted and it seemed safe to venture back. What devastation! The pool, a mud hole; the grove, a shambles; the cave, blocked. The oracle—I had no idea whether she was alive or dead, walled up in her cave. In any case, I could not enter to find out.

"There shattered my first and best hope," said Fronto. "I confess, my dear Lucian, I sank down and wept as never jackass wept before."

Fronto shuddered and sighed miserably at the recollection. Lucian put a comforting arm around the poet's neck. "There must be some way of getting you back to yourself again."

"An idea uppermost in my mind," said Fronto. "I might go so far as to call it a preoccupation on the verge of obsession. The prospect of remaining forever a jackass is enough to take up one's undivided attention.

"Since the oracle herself was unavailable, I decided on the next best thing: to seek out a wise-woman, a healer who might have knowledge of such matters.

"Accordingly, I set off across country, hoping for a road that would lead me to some nearby village. I had not gone far when I glimpsed three rough-looking fellows squatting around a cook fire. They were as villainous a lot as I'd ever seen, all my instincts warned me to keep clear of them.

"Regrettably, they caught sight of me at the same time I caught sight of them. Before I could turn aside, they jumped to their feet and raced after me. One seized me by the mane, another by the tail; and, no matter how I kicked and struggled, they held me fast.

" 'Oho, what's this?' cried the third. 'A wandering jackass! Just what we need.'

"Next thing I knew, I was tethered to a tree. At first, I considered speaking up and explaining that I was no jackass at all; but I thought better of it, fearing these ruffians would take me for some freak of nature, and no telling what they might do.

"So, I held my tongue until I could take stock of my situation. They did not hold theirs, talking openly among themselves as if I were a dumb beast. I listened in growing dismay, for they were plotting no less than robbery and murder.

"There was, I gathered, a corn dealer, Kroton, living on his country estate not far from here. It was whispered about that he kept sacks of gold squirreled away under his floorboards. These villains intended burglarizing him. After dispatching him and his servants, they would require means of carrying off the heavy sacks and any other valuables. My accidental arrival resolved this difficulty, for it was I who would bear the burden of their ill-gotten gains.

"They, and I with them, kept hidden until deepest dark of night. Goading me along, whacking me whenever

I tried to hold back, they stopped in the forecourt of the house. The vile scheme they were about to undertake outraged my every moral fiber, conscience, and scruples—furthermore, the despicable criminals had neither fed nor watered me—and I formed a plan I hoped would defeat them, at possible risk to myself, though with possible gain, as well.

"While one stood guard outside, holding me at a rope's end, his disgusting companions cleverly and silently sprung open the door. Now, for me, came the crucial moment. As soon as the pair disappeared inside the house, I suddenly reared up, kicking and bucking, shouting at the top of my voice: 'Help, ho! Murder! Robbery! Come, friends, all ten of you. Trap them within. Don't let them escape, strike them down without mercy!'

"The first result of my outburst was to startle and terrify the robber beside me, and he dashed off with never a thought for his comrades. The second result was to rouse Kroton and his household and to alarm the robbers, who believed themselves ambushed. They raced from the house, the servants at their heels.

"Kroton himself now appeared, wrapped in his night linen and brandishing a butcher knife. Having urged his servants to pursue the robbers, he turned to me.

" 'Those villains may escape,' he raged, 'but not you,

their accomplice. I'll have my revenge if not on them at least on you.'

"Eager to vent his wrath even on an innocent animal, he started toward me with every intention of cutting my throat.

" 'Stop, stop!' I exclaimed. 'It was I who gave the outcry that saved your life and your gold.'

"Indeed, he halted in his tracks, dumbfounded. Confident of his gratitude and assistance, I hastened to assure him I was the harmless victim of a great misfortune and implored his help. He gradually calmed, and when I finished, he scratched his head, studied me shrewdly, and declared: 'A remarkable, incredible tale. If I didn't know I was awake, I'd think I was asleep. Have no fear, let me consider what best to do for you.'

"Before the servants came back, he warned me against speaking to anyone but himself and led me to an empty grain shed where I impatiently spent the rest of the night looking forward to what he would do to help me.

"In the morning, Kroton returned. He put a halter around my neck and instructed me to come with him to the village adjoining his property. My heart leaped, for I assumed he would take me to the local wise-woman; but, when I told him this, he laughed and said: 'I'll have no dealings with those frightful crones. No, my fine fellow, you're going to make a fortune. For me, that is.'

"When we arrived at the little marketplace, the meaning of Kroton's unsettling words became all too clear.

" 'Gather round,' he called out to the local idlers and passersby. 'Come and hear the amazing talking jackass, the only one of his kind in the world. With utmost patience, I've taught the brute to speak, which he does with greatest eloquence. Do you doubt it?' Kroton continued while the crowd burst out in cries of disbelief. 'I'll wager money on the truth of what I claim.'

" 'And I'll wager all in my purse that you're hoaxing us,' retorted a bystander, flinging down a number of silver coins. The others followed his example, eager to wager that Kroton was trying to trick them.

" 'Don't you contradict me,' Kroton muttered in my ear. 'Do as you're told or so much the worse for you. Now, go on. Say something. Recite one of your verses, lacking anything better.'

"Outraged by Kroton's treachery and ingratitude, determined to have my revenge, I only wheezed and heehawed like any common ass.

"At this, the crowd began hooting and jeering, accusing Kroton of being a liar or out of his wits. They picked up their money and demanded that he pay off his part of the wager.

" 'He can speak, he can speak as well as any of

you,' protested Kroton. 'I had a talk with him only this morning.'

"While the crowd threatened bodily harm if he reneged, Kroton pummeled and kicked me, shaking his fist, ordering me to prove him right. I, however, stood mute as a stone.

" 'I warned you,' shouted Kroton. 'Treacherous poet! To the knacker's yard, to the slaughterhouse with you! I'll have the hide off your back for a rug and boil your hooves into glue, and get that much from you, in any case.'

" 'Hold on there,' put in a rough-bearded man— Cerdo, as I later learned. 'That's wasting a perfectly serviceable jackass. I need a pack beast, and I'll give you enough to make good on what you owe these folk before they take you yourself to the knacker.'

" 'Done and done!' returned Kroton, snatching Cerdo's cash with one hand and giving him my halter with the other. 'Take him away. Beat him within an inch of his life and beyond, for all I care. Never again will I trust a poet.'

"So it was," concluded Fronto, "that I fell into the clutches of Cerdo. He subjected me to the painful indignity of branding his mark on my rump with a red hot iron, setting the seal of my slavery to him. From then on, my life at the hands of that brute was nothing but cudgeling, starvation, endless toil—a donkey's a sturdy creature, but with such mistreatment my days were surely numbered. Until you, my dear Lucian, set me free; for which I am eternally grateful.

"But here," Fronto added, "our ways must part: I, to keep on with my search; you, wherever your own road leads. I'm too sentimental a fellow for long good-byes, so let us simply take brief but fond leave of each other. I wish you the best of good fortune. Should you ever meet another donkey, I trust you'll do as well for him as you've done for me. You never know who he might be."

5

Joy-in-the-Dance

W ait," Lucian called as Fronto started from the clearing. "You can't roam around by yourself. You'll be grabbed again. I'll stay with you until we find a healer."

"A generous offer," said Fronto, "but you have your own troubles. You're not the most popular fellow in Arkadia. If those soothsayers lay hold of you, they'll carve you like one of their chickens. Also, you made off with Cerdo's property and he's a vengeful sort. You'd best find some backwater hamlet and quietly hole up there. I'll manage. As a poet, I'm accustomed to the seamy side of life."

"You're a donkey now," said Lucian.

"You have a point," said Fronto, "and even a poet must occasionally bow to logic. Yes, I'll be grateful for your company. Come, then. I suggest we find whatever poor excuse for a road they have in these parts."

Fronto picked his way through the undergrowth and struck on a path leading away from Metara. Lucian, at first, kept glancing over his shoulder, as if Calchas, Phobos, and Cerdo were about to pounce on him at any moment. As the morning wore on, however, he began striding more lightheartedly. He laughed at a gray squirrel sitting on its haunches, forepaws folded, looking like one of the old palace archivists. He glimpsed a hard-shelled beetle armored like a warrior. He had never heard such chirping and whistling as he heard from the many different birds in the woods. But what fascinated him most was his companion trotting along beside him.

At last he ventured to ask, "Fronto, tell me. How did you get to be a poet?"

"I haven't the least notion," replied Fronto. "I didn't get to be; I always was. As I wrote in one of my elegies: 'Poets are born, not made.' It isn't something you acquire like a skin rash."

"That's all there is to it?"

"Certainly not. One should learn the nature of odes, anthems, apostrophes, and so on. And, of course, the proper use of metaphor, simile, metathesis, just to begin.

"Then, epithets, your nice little ready-made phrases: rosy-fingered dawn, sandy shores, wine-dark seas.

They've been stock-in-trade for time out of mind."

"You don't have to think them up?"

"Originality?" Fronto shuddered. "Heavens, no. Why risk upsetting anyone? These are tried and true, sure to please. You can cobble up whole epics from them. Next, the matter of rhyme schemes, rhythmics, dactyls, anapests, spondees—"

"You know all that?"

"Of course not. I only mean one should. If I ever escape this ridiculous carcass, I might devote a little time to studying them. They do come in handy. Prose, however, is a different piece of business. Tales, anecdotes, narratives. All quite simple. Any fool can tell a story. Take a few odds and ends of things that happen to you, dress them up, shuffle them about, add a dash of excitement, a little color, and there you have it."

"You could tell the story of your turning into a jackass," Lucian said. "That's an amazing tale just as it is."

"No," said Fronto. "Too bizarre, grotesque, unpleasant. But, to give you an example, I could build a tale from, say, the moment I looked into the pool. Instead of me, it would be a handsome fellow, a conceited young fop who gazes so closely at his own reflection that he falls in and drowns. Instead of an ass, he's transformed into—oh, some kind of beautiful flower. That's more charming than a donkey and would go down better with the audience. And—ah, yes, he has a sweetheart who pines away until she's a mere shadow of herself. I'd have to work it out, but you grasp the method."

"Here's a good idea for you," said Lucian. "How I found a mistake in my inventories and had to run off before Calchas and Phobos got hold of me."

"Boring," said Fronto. "Forgive me, I'm yawning already. Conflict, struggle, suspense—that's what's needed to make a tale move along. You don't just run off. They seize you. You fight them with all your strength, almost win; but they bind you hand and foot, get ready to chop you up with meat cleavers. You escape in the nick of time. I don't know how. That's a technical detail."

"It didn't happen that way," Lucian protested.

"My point exactly," said Fronto. "All the more reason to spice it up. The meat cleavers are an especially nice touch."

"But it wouldn't be true."

"Not important," said Fronto. "If a storyteller worried about the facts—my dear Lucian, how could he ever get at the truth?"

❧

Over the next several days, Lucian began to despair of finding a wise-woman. In some hamlets, the folk were devoted to the Lady; they would have helped him, but the local healers had fled, no one knew where. In other villages, the dwellers belonged to the Bear tribe; the men scorned anything to do with the Lady and drove him off with curses, plus a few rocks to speed him on his way.

One afternoon, he stopped in a village to buy food with the last of his coins. Smarting from previous welcomes, he was cautious and roundabout in asking information. Prepared for yet another disappointment, he was happily surprised when the shopkeeper drew him aside and whispered that an old wise-woman lived on a patch of farmland only a league down the road.

Needing to hear no more, Lucian ran from the shop. So far, he had walked beside Fronto, feeling it was somehow disrespectful to ride on a poet. Now, while the shopkeeper kept waving and shouting after him, he jumped on Fronto's back and they set off at a gallop.

He found the place easily enough and smelled it before he saw it. Smoke billowed from the windows. The farmhouse roof blazed. Warriors were thrusting torches into sheds and outbuildings. Fronto reared in alarm. Lucian tumbled off. By the time he scrambled to his feet, the troop captain had ridden up to him.

"You." The officer pointed a short-bladed sword. He was a burly man, sweating in a leather breastplate, his helmet tilted on the back of his head. "What's your business here?"

Lucian stared. The buildings were past saving, along with anyone inside. The shopkeeper, he realized, had tried to warn him.

"Who are you?" The captain leaned from the saddle and squinted at Lucian. "Let's have a better look." He climbed down and gripped Lucian's shirtfront. "I've seen that face before. Where? Metara? The palace?"

"Me? In a palace? Don't I wish it." Lucian smiled innocently, trying to keep himself from shaking with fright at the same time. "I'm going to visit my Uncle Dimitrios. He's laid up with rheumatism something terrible. The dampness, you see, when the roof started leaking. He needs someone—"

"Leave off all that. You tell me quick: What do you want with the old hag that lived here?"

"Sir, I lost my way. I turned off to ask directions. I don't know anything about hags."

"Good thing you don't," said the officer, shoving him aside. "All right, clear out. On foot, my lad. One of my pack mules pulled up lame. I need a fresh one. This jackass is officially commandeered. He's a royal ass now.

"Throw a rope on the beast," the captain ordered two of his warriors. "Take him to the village. We're done here."

"Get your hands off him." Lucian flung himself against the nearest warrior and sent him stumbling back;

then spun around to grapple with the other. Fronto bucked and shied away. Lucian flailed wildly with his fists, pummeling so furiously that his bewildered opponent lost his balance and dropped to one knee. Darting to Fronto's side, Lucian swung a leg over the poet's haunches.

The troop captain, shrugging as if obliged to deal with a tiresome hindrance, brought up his sword and launched a sweeping, backhanded blow. Struck with the flat of the blade, Lucian pitched to the ground, stunned out of his wits.

By the time he remembered how to operate his arms and legs, the warriors were already far down the road. He lurched after them, shaking his fists and hurling threats. He managed only half a dozen floundering steps before tumbling down again.

"I saw them take your donkey," remarked a light voice behind him. "Let's see what damage they did to you."

Lucian turned to stare into the gray eyes of a slender, long-legged girl, her braided hair the color of ripe wheat. She stood, hands on hips, observing him with concern, curiosity, and a little glint of wry amusement. At sight of her, Lucian felt some difficulty catching his breath. Despite a sudden giddiness, he straightened up, squared his shoulders, and hoped to give the impression that he was sitting on the turf only because he wanted to.

"I was watching from the bushes," the girl went on. "That officer gave you quite a whack."

"I'd have given him worse," Lucian retorted. "Sneaking coward. He hit me when I wasn't looking."

"The most sensible time to do it, from his viewpoint. Just be glad you're not missing a head. Here, swallow this. You'll feel better."

From the cloak slung around her shoulders, the girl produced a small phial and poured the contents into Lucian's mouth, then knelt to examine the result of the sword blow.

"I was looking for the wise-woman." Lucian grimaced at the bitter taste of the liquid. "Someone told me she lives here."

"Not anymore. She was warned in time. She's safe away. As I'll be, once I'm done with you."

"Are you a healer?"

"That depends on what needs healing. In your case, not much. I'm called Joy-in-the-Dance. And you?"

"Aiee! Ouch!" cried Lucian as her fingers probed a tender spot behind his ear.

"Odd name." The girl gave a teasing grin. "Well, then, Aiee-Ouch, you'll mend. Put cold water on that lump. Nothing more to be done."

"The healer's not for me. For my donkey."

"Your donkey's gone. Or don't you remember?"

"I'll get him back. No matter what I have to do. They took him to the village. I'm going after him."

"And then? Knock down the whole troop? Not likely. You'd do better to find another. There's no shortage of donkeys."

"He's not a donkey," Lucian snapped. "He's my friend. I mean, my friend's a donkey now. But he's not himself. He used to be himself—"

"I think I gave you too much of that willow extract," the girl said.

"He needs a wise-woman, a healer, anyone who can help him."

"He's sick? What with?"

"Not sick. He's fine. No, he isn't. He's a poet. Was a poet."

"So far," said Joy-in-the-Dance, "you're making no sense at all. Start with this: Who are you? That shouldn't be too difficult. Once you've managed that, you might get around to telling me how your poetic donkey comes into it."

"My name's Lucian. When I was in the palace, in Metara—"

"What?" burst out Joy-in-the-Dance. "You're one of

the king's people? Spying for Bromios? Hunting down wise-women? I should have left you to mend your own head."

"No, no," Lucian broke in. "I ran away. I had to. They'd have murdered me."

"I'll do worse than that if you don't give me some better answers."

"I'm trying to explain," Lucian flung back. "You keep mixing me up. We're here because Fronto—the donkey —had an accident when he was a poet."

"Aiee-Ouch, I'm running out of patience."

"How it began, you see, before I met Fronto—" Lucian hesitated. Something peculiar was happening to him. Facing this wheat-haired, gray-eyed girl, he suddenly felt, among other sensations, that he was a very dull fellow, with his dull beans and dull inventories. It became urgently important to put himself in a more interesting light, as any young man in his position would have done.

So, recalling Fronto's advice about storytelling, he cleared his throat and offered the following account.

6

The Invisible Dinner

I was chief scribe in the king's great palace high above
the sandy shores of the wine-dark sea," said Lucian.
"One day, at rosy-fingered dawn, my duties took me into
a storeroom to count—to inspect, that is—tall jars of oil.
I was just coming from behind a row of these jars when
the royal soothsayers, Calchas and Phobos, entered, and,
with them, one of the provisioners to the royal household, a merchant named Cerdo.

"Unaware of my presence, they were talking intently
among themselves. I could not help overhearing their
conversation, and I was shocked and horrified; for I
quickly understood that they were scheming to steal
huge sums of money from the palace treasury.

"Not daring to move, I listened with mounting indignation at such dishonesty and treachery; and grew so agitated that my foot scraped against one of the jars. At this, Cerdo broke off and scowled villainously.

" 'Hark,' he whispered, furtively glancing around. 'What's that noise? Are you sure we're alone?'

" 'Only a rat,' replied Calchas. 'The place is crawling with them.'

" 'Yes,' I thought, 'and I see three of them right there.' I pressed closer behind the jars; but, amid the dust and spiderwebs, I began sneezing violently.

" 'A rat?' burst out Cerdo. 'Next, you'll tell me he'll blow his nose.'

"Seeing no other course, I boldly sprang from my hiding place. 'Your vile conspiracy is exposed!' I exclaimed. 'You are no better than common thieves and deserve to be treated as such.'

"At first, they cringed in terror, knowing their criminal wrongdoing would cost their lives. They begged me to keep their secret, promising a share of their ill-gotten gains in exchange for my silence. This offer, naturally, I refused.

"Overcoming their alarm, they realized that they were three against one, and they all set upon me. As much as I fought and struggled, they overpowered and bound me hand and foot with ropes. Next, they lifted me up and put me into one of the jars.

" 'There you stay, my fine fellow,' said Calchas, 'until we come back and decide how best to dispose of you.'

"What was I to do? Imprisoned in an oil jar, my life hanging in the balance, I nevertheless remained calm and sought a way to release myself. I quickly discovered the means. Some oil was still in the bottom of the jar. I soaked the ropes in it, covering hands and feet with the substance. This lubrication allowed me to slip free of my bonds.

"However, no sooner had I climbed out of the jar than Calchas and Phobos returned; in their hands were sharp, glittering meat cleavers.

"Seeing me about to escape, the villains pursued me all around the storeroom, brandishing their murderous cleavers and vowing to chop me into a hundred pieces. Dodging Calchas, I was nearly overtaken by Phobos; spinning away from Phobos, I strove to elude Calchas. Step by step, inch by inch, they pressed me closer and closer. Another instant and I would be hopelessly trapped. Calchas raised his cleaver, about to bring it down on my head.

"The gleaming blade whistled through the air. In the nick of time, even as the fearsome weapon was no more than a hair's breadth away, I sprang through a window, raced across the courtyard, scaled the wall, and dropped to the other side.

"By good fortune, a donkey happened to be standing at that very spot. I landed astride—"

"Stop," Joy-in-the-Dance broke in. "Enough."

"It's a terrifying scene," said Lucian. "I'm sorry if it upset you."

"It didn't," said Joy-in-the-Dance. "It's ridiculous. The most preposterous tissue of nonsense I've ever heard."

"It's true," protested Lucian. "Almost. Some of it. The facts—yes, all right, a little different. They're not important. Fronto himself told me so."

"You take advice from a jackass?"

"He's a poet. I'm trying to explain—"

"Save your breath," said Joy-in-the-Dance. "First, you claim you need help, then you come out with some absurd fabrication. I don't know what you're up to and I don't think I want to. I certainly don't want to be fobbed off with meat cleavers and oil jars and jumping out of windows. If you're going to lie, at least be convincing. Good-bye. I have things to do."

"I thought you were a healer," Lucian burst out as the girl turned away. "You're supposed to help people, aren't you? Never mind, then. Go on, walk off. Good-bye yourself. I don't care if you believe it or not, but my friend got changed into a donkey and that's a fact."

Joy-in-the-Dance turned and strode back to him.

"What did you say? Changed into—is that more of your nonsense?"

"It's exactly what happened," Lucian retorted. The girl's eyes were fixed on his own, as if she were trying to peer through them into the nooks and crannies of his brain. He had the uncomfortable impression that she might be succeeding.

Joy-in-the-Dance said nothing for a few moments, then stretched out a finger to prod Lucian's chest. "Listen to me, Aiee-Ouch—"

"My name's Lucian."

"Yes. Well, listen to me, Aiee-Ouch. If you're spinning out another tale, I'll be very unhappy with you. But I'm going to assume there's a grain of truth in all this."

"A grain? Thank you for believing that much. Do you mind telling me how you'll make sure?"

"Simple. I'll go and ask your friend."

"Oh? As easy as that?" Lucian said wryly. "If you didn't think I could get to him, I don't see how you will. You? A girl?"

"You noticed? That was clever of you." Joy-in-the-Dance smiled. "Yes, Aiee-Ouch, I'll be interested in having a few words with your jackass."

Joy-in-the-Dance beckoned him to a sheltered spot away from the smoldering farmhouse. There, she sat cross-legged, folded her hands, and lowered her eyes.

"What are you doing?" cried Lucian. "You said we were going after Fronto."

"We are. At the right time. Meanwhile, I'm sleeping. Or was, until you interrupted."

"You sleep sitting up? Like a chicken? I never heard of such a thing."

"You Bear people wouldn't know how. It's a little knack we learn when we're children; and it's more comfortable than sprawling on the ground—like a stunned ox. You'd be wise to get some rest, too, instead of flapping around."

The girl took a deep breath and again shut her eyes. Lucian paced back and forth, chafing at the delay, impatient to reach Fronto. At last, he gave in to weariness and sank down with his knees drawn up and his head resting on them. Long after moonrise, Joy-in-the-Dance leisurely climbed to her feet and motioned for Lucian to follow.

Stepping quickly and quietly, they reached the village just before dawn. The little marketplace was empty, nothing stirred. Lucian would have clung cautiously to the shadows, but the girl walked straight to the inn and glanced through a window.

"Good," she whispered. "The captain and his louts have stuffed themselves and swilled everything they could find. An earthquake wouldn't rouse them. That's why I waited."

"They'll have sentries on watch."

The girl shrugged. She beckoned Lucian to the rear of the inn, where an open-fronted shed served as a stable. Amid the tethered pack animals, a guard squatted, head nodding, a guttering lantern beside him. Lucian glimpsed Fronto, ears woefully drooping.

"Stay here," said Joy-in-the-Dance as Lucian started forward. She went boldly to the guard, who roused and reached for his sword.

"Put that away. You don't need it," Joy-in-the-Dance said reassuringly. "I brought you something. Just what you've been wanting. See here. Look. Look close."

The girl made a few quick motions at the sentry. "A roasted partridge. It smells delicious. Done to a turn. Your mouth's watering for it, you're so hungry. Go on, eat your fill."

Lucian saw nothing whatever in the girl's out-stretched hands. Yet the sentry's face lit up, he licked his lips, and put his fingers to his mouth as if he were cram-ming in morsels of food.

"It tastes so good." Joy-in-the-Dance nodded approval while the man chewed and gulped empty air. "You'll want something to wash it down."

Again, she held out her hands. "A big pitcher of what

you like best. Drink up, don't stint yourself. You deserve a little refreshment, sitting here all night.

"It's strong," she went on as the guard made a show of swigging from an invisible vessel. "Oh, I'm afraid it's gone to your head. Spinning round and round. Tipsy, are you? Yes. Very tipsy. No matter, you'll sleep it off. Now."

At this, the guard swayed on his feet and sat down heavily, belching and snoring, lost to the world.

"What did you do?" Lucian gasped. "There's no partridge. No pitcher of drink. How—?"

"Don't babble, Aiee-Ouch. Go fetch your donkey."

Lucian darted into the shed, warned the poet to be silent, and hastily untethered him.

"Let's get out of here," said Joy-in-the-Dance. "That sentry's going to wake up soon—with a pounding head and a bad case of indigestion."

The girl moved quietly and calmly across the marketplace, Lucian and Fronto behind her. Once out of the village, she headed into the woodlands, setting such a brisk pace that Lucian wondered if she could see in the dark as well as conjure up roasted fowl. It was sunrise by the time she halted.

"Very well," she said. "Here's your donkey. What does he have to say for himself?"

"Who are you? What are you?" murmured Lucian.

"You cast some kind of spell back there. I've heard tales of that." He drew back uneasily. "Are you a girl at all?"

"I should hope so. And I didn't cast a spell. I only suggested what the guard wanted and he did the rest himself. You might thank me for saving your jackass instead of gaping like an idiot; but, never mind, I want to hear him talk."

"It's all right," Lucian said to Fronto. "Joy-in-the-Dance is—claims—she's a healer."

"Blessings on you, my dear young woman." Fronto tossed his head. "I'm delighted beyond words to make your acquaintance."

"He does talk," the girl said to Lucian. "That much is true."

"You're not surprised?" said Fronto.

"Why should I be? Every animal talks. I admit you're the first jackass I've met who uses human speech, but being able to talk is less important than being able to talk sense. Your friend has difficulty along those lines. So, you tell me straight out what happened."

"Once you hear my sad history," said Fronto, "I have no doubt that you'll be moved by those emotions I conveyed in one of my finest odes: pity and terror."

"In that case," said Joy-in-the-Dance, "keep it mercifully short."

Fronto quickly repeated his account, concluding with

his misadventure in the pool. Instead of pity and terror, the girl displayed what Lucian had to judge as fury. She seized Fronto by the ears and began shaking him until his teeth rattled.

"You drank? You swam?" she burst out. "How dare you—"

"Let him be!" Lucian sprang to protect the belabored poet. "You're supposed to cure him, not batter him to pieces." He tussled with Joy-in-the-Dance, who was much stronger than he expected; at last he pulled her away. She and Lucian fell back, out of breath and glaring at each other.

"He meant no harm," declared Lucian. "He wanted to go to the pythoness and beg forgiveness. It's not his fault if the warriors attacked the sanctuary and walled her up.

"As for that," Lucian hurried on, "the pythoness herself started all the trouble. If she hadn't given Bromios that prophecy to begin with, there'd have been no attack. Or farmhouses burned, wise-women hunted down, or anything else. Fronto might have made a little mistake, but it's the pythoness who's responsible for the trouble he's in now."

"Oh, yes, twist everything around," Joy-in-the-Dance snapped back. "To be expected from a man, and one of the Bear tribe into the bargain."

"Bear tribe or not, that's how I see it," Lucian retorted. "I'm sorry for what happened to her, but I wish she could know what a mess she began."

"She does." The girl's eyes flashed. "I'm Woman-Who-Talks-to-Snakes."

7

Mysteries of Women

M y dear girl," Fronto said as Lucian's jaw dropped, "the oracle has resided in her cave from time immemorial. In which case, you'd be as ancient as Mount Lerna itself. Clearly—and charmingly, I hasten to add—you are noticeably younger. I'm grateful for whatever assistance you gave my friend here, but you can hardly expect us to believe—"

"Fronto, I don't know who she is or what she is," Lucian murmured, "but she's the one who rescued you. She did it all. That business with the partridge—"

"Was a bird involved?" said Fronto. "Did I miss something? I was deep in unhappy thoughts, paying no attention until the moment you untied me. How did a partridge come into it?"

"Never mind, I'll explain later." Lucian paused and shook his head. "I don't see how it's possible, but is there any way she could be telling the truth? She can do amazing things. I've seen that for myself."

"I quite understand," replied Fronto, "that any lad would be eager to believe whatever an attractive young woman chooses to tell him. Only apply a little reason and common sense. The oracle was walled up in the cave. We must presume she perished there."

"When the two of you decide whether I'm old as the hills or dead as a mackerel," said Joy-in-the-Dance, "I'll be interested in your conclusions. As for you, Aiee-Ouch, I'm delighted to hear one of you Bear men admit that a girl can do anything at all. It must have felt like having your skin peeled off.

"As for you," she added to Fronto, "you're a poet, so apply a little imagination. Did it ever cross your mind that there could be another way out of the cave? Or more than one pythoness? Oracles don't live forever. There were dozens before me.

"I served the last one. She taught me her lore and learning. When she died this winter, I was chosen to take her place. I'm not used to having my word questioned; but, for the sake of ending the discussion—"

From beneath her tunic she drew out a medallion on a silver chain: the figure of a woman crowned with a tall headdress and holding a serpent in each hand. "Here. The emblem of Woman-Who-Talks-to-Snakes. Only a pythoness may wear it."

Fronto stared a moment, then burst out: "Revered oracle! Venerated pythoness! I humbly apologize for doubting. And let me add that I wholeheartedly deplore the disaster that's come upon you."

"Disaster, yes, it's every bit of that," Joy-in-the-Dance said, her features tightening. "The Lady's devotees are hunted down, their lives at stake. I've seen to it that my maidens are safe in hiding, and as many others as I could reach. I sent away the healer at the farm. Right now, that's the best I can do. Which isn't much in the way of settling things.

"Aiee-Ouch was right," she added bitterly. "My prophecy started the whole mess—as he was very quick to point out."

"I didn't mean to put it quite that way," said Lucian.

"It's true, no matter how you put it," Joy-in-the-Dance said. "I knew there'd be trouble for sure, but it turned out worse than I foresaw."

"Couldn't you have changed the prophecy?" asked Lucian. "Made it a little easier for Bromios to swallow? Or thought up something different?"

"You don't think up a prophecy. It comes to you. First, it isn't there; then, there it is. The same way, I suppose, that a poem comes to mind. I can't explain it. Fronto should know what I mean."

"Indeed I do," said Fronto, "though it hasn't happened to me lately."

"But—yes, I thought of changing it." The girl's face fell. "I wanted to. It was my first prophecy. It frightened me. I couldn't understand what it meant. I didn't want to be the one who pronounced it. I was tempted a dozen times to put it aside. Who'd have known? Not Bromios. I could have told him any sort of harmless nonsense and that would have been the end of it.

"I even wondered if it was false, or if I'd misunderstood. Until the moment Bromios set foot in the cave, I still wasn't sure what to do."

The girl's chin went up, in pride and defiance; but Lucian saw tears glinting in her eyes. "Then I decided I couldn't turn away from what I had to tell him. I spoke the prophecy as it had come to me. Now that I see what it brought on us"—she glanced down and shook her head—"I'm not sure if I did right or wrong."

"I'm not the one to say," Lucian admitted. "I don't know about such mysteries. I just count beans. What I do know—what I didn't realize before—you risked your life rescuing Fronto in the midst of the king's warriors. They're hunting the pythoness everywhere."

"They think she's an old hag," said Joy-in-the-Dance.

"Do I fit that description? But you and Fronto shouldn't linger. I'll miss my guess if the captain doesn't send his men out searching."

"They won't go to that much trouble for a missing donkey."

"Not for a donkey. For me. The guard's bound to report what happened. The captain isn't altogether stupid. Even a Bear warrior has brains enough to reckon that anyone who makes a roasted partridge appear out of thin air is worth some close questioning.

"Let them look for me. They won't find me. I'll set so many false trails they won't know which way they're going. It will keep them off your track, too. They'll be so busy they won't think about following you."

"You're not leaving—"

"Yes, I'm afraid I have to. Good-bye—Lucian." She grinned at him. "No. Aiee-Ouch suits you better."

"Stop! Stop!" burst out Fronto. "You're forgetting something most important: changing me back to myself."

"Fronto, I'm truly sorry for you," the girl said. "I wish I could do as you ask."

"But surely you can," said Lucian. "You speak prophecies, conjure up partridges and who knows what else; you can sleep like a chicken—"

"Adorable pythoness!" exclaimed Fronto, in growing alarm and dismay. "Turning an ass into a man—what effort would it take, with all those powers? Hardly enough to raise a sweat."

"It doesn't work that way," the girl said patiently. "Let me explain. No one, these days, has magical powers. Not even I."

"Oh?" Fronto snorted. "Then what happened to me?"

"I'm trying to tell you. We don't have magical powers. The powers we do have are useful, but they aren't magical. All of us devoted to the Lady learn about healing herbs, the movement of the stars telling when to plant and reap. How to find water underground. We understand the speech of animals—but only because we watch and listen and know their ways. And a lot more, besides. All perfectly natural. You men call them 'women's mysteries' because we keep them to ourselves. We don't share them with men, Bear men least of all."

"How can you not?" interrupted Lucian. "These are marvelous things for everybody."

"We don't trust you men with them," said Joy-in-the-Dance. "Thickheaded oafs like Bromios? Worse yet, that pair of greedy soothsayers? They're vicious and ruthless, beneath all their oiliness. They'd twist that knowledge to their own purposes. They'd use it to kill and destroy. We women won't let that happen."

"If you don't mind my saying," put in Fronto, "you're straying from the point."

"No, I'm explaining the point," said Joy-in-the-Dance. "The pool at Mount Lerna was truly magical. There used to be other magical places—groves of trees, rings of standing stones, fountains. That was long ago, when real enchanters lived here. The Bear tribe destroyed most of those places to build towns and villages. The magic simply faded away from the others. The pool was the last. Now it's gone, too. As for you, Fronto, magic changed you into a jackass. Only magic can change you back."

"You just told me it's all gone," wailed Fronto. "I'm a jackass forever. Send me to the knacker! Fling me into a river! Anything to end this asinine existence!"

Joy-in-the-Dance laid a calming hand on Fronto's neck. "There's still a chance. One person might help you: the Lady of Wild Things."

"How can she?" put in Lucian. "She isn't real, she's just an old wives' tale."

"That's what you Bear men think. Believe me, she's very real. She lives on the north coast, in her sanctuary at Mount Panthea."

"If that's true—all right, yes, I'll believe you," said Lucian. "I'll take Fronto there. Can you tell me how to find the sanctuary?"

"I can," said the girl. "I can also tell you it's forbidden to men of the Bear tribe. And that, I'm sure, includes jackasses. You couldn't set foot anywhere close to the place."

Fronto, having brightened for a moment, looked more dismal than ever. "No use, then. My dear Lucian, do me one last good turn."

"Wait a minute. Let me think," said Joy-in-the-Dance. "There might be a way around that rule. I can speak on your behalf. I'm going to Mount Panthea. I have to see the Lady of Wild Things."

8

Forbidden Enchantments

You have my undying gratitude!" exclaimed Fronto. "I'll dedicate a hymn of thanksgiving to you—once I'm in a position to do so."

"Don't thank me yet," said Joy-in-the-Dance. "Even the Lady might not be able to help. Whether she can— that's one thing. Whether she will—that's another. You committed a serious offense, Fronto. She could decide it served you right and leave you as you are; or lay on a worse punishment."

"I hadn't thought of that," said Fronto, "but my considered opinion is: Anything's better than what I am."

"And I—" Lucian began, "I wonder if the Lady might help me, too? If Calchas and Phobos get their hands on me, they'll kill me. I don't dare go back to the palace or anywhere they could find me. What can I do? Hide away in some hole and corner for the rest of my life? Count beans forever? No, that's over and done with. Fronto was a poet. He'll be one again, if the Lady transforms him. But I? What could I be? I haven't been anything much in the first place. Would the Lady tell me?"

"Aiee-Ouch, you do astonish me," Joy-in-the-Dance said. "People have implored her for riches, fame, magical secrets, and whatever else you could imagine—without getting them, naturally. But wanting to know what to do with your life? I've never heard of such a request. If she's willing to see you, you'll have to ask her yourself.

"I hadn't bargained on traveling companions," she added, "least of all a donkey and an Aiee-Ouch; but I dread to think of you two blundering about on your own. Yes, I'll take you to Mount Panthea. You have to keep pace, though. No wandering off, poking into things that aren't your business, making a nuisance—"

"Agreed most happily!" exclaimed Fronto.

"You're the pythoness." Lucian turned away and grumbled under his breath to Fronto, "Pythoness or not, she doesn't have to give me lessons in common sense. I'm no child. I'm a man, after all."

"Yes, exactly," said Joy-in-the-Dance, whose ears were keener than Lucian supposed. "Now, let's be away from here or we'll have a pack of warriors on our heels."

The girl set off, with Lucian and Fronto scrambling after her. For the rest of the morning, however, Lucian saw little of their guide. She was continually leaving them to wait while she disappeared into the brush, reappearing later from a different direction; or circling, or doubling back on her own footsteps. Once, she popped up without her cloak, explaining she had dropped it where the troop would surely find it; another time, her cheeks and knees were crisscrossed with bramble scratches, her braid had come undone, and she looked thoroughly pleased.

"That," she remarked, brushing twigs from her hair, "will do nicely. They'll end up chasing one another."

If Lucian had been nettled by the girl taking her authority for granted, over the next few days he grudgingly admitted to himself that he would have been lost, famished, bone sore, and parched without her. Joy-in-the-Dance was always able to pick the easiest pathways and most comfortable sleeping spots. She found hidden springs of clear water, unearthed odd-shaped edible roots, dug out nuts the squirrels had buried: meager fare, but it staved off hunger and thirst.

One day, she found a honey tree. While Lucian and Fronto kept a safe distance, the girl calmly walked straight to it and began a high-pitched, wordless singing. The bees swarmed from the hollow trunk and formed a starlike crown on her head. Still singing, she reached into the hive and broke off a portion of honeycomb. As she stepped away, the bees streamed back into their tree.

"How—? What did you do?" stammered Lucian. "Or is that a woman's mystery?"

"Only a small one."

"No use, then, asking you to teach me," Lucian said wryly. "All right, I can understand why you don't share your secrets with Bear people like Bromios, or soothsayers like Calchas and Phobos. But I'm not the Bear tribe, I'm only me. Besides, I've heard that a lot of Bear men are devoted to the Lady. They won't turn your mysteries against you."

"How do we know?" said Joy-in-the-Dance. "We can't be sure what they'd do once they had that kind of knowledge. We won't take the risk. We decided that long ago. We have a tale about it, handed down from mother to daughter—"

"A story?" broke in Lucian, pricking up his ears. "Would you tell that to me, at least? I've never heard anything but Bear lore."

"Not surprising. No wonder you're an Aiee-Ouch."

Though Lucian pressed her to tell him, she said no more on the subject, leaving him disappointed and more than a little vexed.

"My boy," Fronto later remarked to him, "I've been observing. I do believe our admirable pythoness has a bit of a soft spot for you. I'm a poet, I detect such things."

Lucian snorted. "Well, I'm not a poet, but what I detect is: Half the time, she doesn't make sense; the other half, she makes me feel like an idiot."

"Precisely," said Fronto. "That's another of those women's mysteries."

That same day, Joy-in-the-Dance halted in a dense corner of the forest and beckoned Lucian and Fronto past the tangled undergrowth.

"It's summer here!" Lucian hardly believed his eyes. A ring of ancient oaks stood in full, rich foliage. Flowering vines clung to the gnarled trunks. Crimson and white blossoms covered the bushes. He took a deep breath of the warm, fragrant air. Only a few paces behind him, the trees had just begun to put out new leaves. "Why here and nowhere else?"

"It stays like this all year-round." Joy-in-the-Dance took his hand and led him to a pool glittering in the sunlight. A ledge of polished marble rimmed the water. Nearby rose a little pavilion; ivy twined to the top of its slender columns. "This used to be one of the magical places I told you about. Most of the magic's gone, but there's still a little bit left. From the days when the Great Ones lived in Arkadia."

"Where are they now? What happened?" Lucian asked. "Can you tell me?"

"Yes. It's something you ought to know. You, too, Fronto. It's about a man meddling with things that didn't concern him." The girl settled cross-legged at the pool's rim. Lucian drew closer to her as she began: "Long ago, before the Bear tribe came to Arkadia, there was a man called Think-Too-Late.

"He had everything he needed. His vines gave him the heaviest bunches of the sweetest grapes. In his orchard, ripe fruits fell into his hands without his climbing to pluck them. When his wife, Giving-All-Gifts, sat at her loom, the cloth wove itself with never a knot or broken thread. Clear water filled his well to the brim, his crops sprang up in abundance, his livestock never sickened, nor did he. For all that, he was restless and unsatisfied."

"How could he be?" put in Lucian. "I don't understand that."

"You will," said Joy-in-the-Dance. "In those days, mighty enchanters lived in Arkadia: the Great Ones. They were tall and graceful, fair of face and generous in spirit, with powers past mortal understanding. One, for instance, Arbikanos, knew the secret of transforming himself into any animal, bird, or sea creature, and back again. Another, Stephanos, knew the opposite art: how to change animals into human beings. Of yet another, Dalbenos, it was said that he could, whenever he chose, start his life afresh as a newborn infant. And there were many more, all gifted with magical skills and knowledge.

"But the most powerful was called Woman-Three-Women, who could take the form of a beautiful maiden, a kindly mother, or a frightful hag. She could spin life-threads, measure, and shear them off. She knew how all things began and ended, and the shape of mortal destinies. The other Great Ones honored her in their sanctuary and council hall at the foot of Mount Panthea.

"It was thanks to these Great Ones that Think-Too-Late, like his fellow mortals, was showered with so many blessings. The enchanters provided for all his needs. They caused his fields to flourish, his animals to thrive, his household to prosper without toil or trouble. Out of their loving kindness, they kept Arkadia a land of peaceful happiness."

"She's setting the scene very nicely for us," remarked Fronto. "Building up the atmosphere. It's no doubt one of those tales of sentiment and tender feelings. The ladies enjoy that sort of thing."

"As for Think-Too-Late," Joy-in-the-Dance went on, ignoring Fronto, "having nothing better to occupy his mind, he began to think about his condition; and, the more he thought about it, the more fault he found.

" 'The Great Ones have given us good things,' he said to his wife. 'All very nice, I admit. But no one with any sense or wisdom gives away everything. So, if the Great Ones have given us this much, they could surely give us more if they chose. Since they haven't given us everything, they're holding something back. And if they're holding something back, it must be most precious. And if it's most precious, I find it mean-spirited and tightfisted of them not to share it.'

"Giving-All-Gifts told him to put that notion out of his mind and be glad for all he had. But Think-Too-Late kept gnawing at it so much that soon it began gnawing at him.

"It had long been rumored that the Great Ones had buried an iron-bound chest at the peak of Mount Panthea. Some whispered that the coffer held a vast treasure; others, that it was filled with magical objects, even the secret of eternal life. Think-Too-Late had never given much credit to this gossip. Now, he believed the rumors must be true.

" 'Whatever's in that box,' he told himself, 'has to be more precious than anyone can imagine, or it wouldn't be hidden. Yes, the Great Ones are holding something back. Since they won't share it freely, I have every reason to go and take it.'

"When Giving-All-Gifts warned that it was not only dangerous but also downright stealing, Think-Too-Late brushed aside her objections. 'Stealing?' he cried. 'How so, when they've given me everything else, why not this? Why should the Great Ones lord it over me, and run my life as they see fit, as if I were a child?'

"Though Giving-All-Gifts pleaded, wept, and wrung her hands, nothing would change his mind. 'Woman,' he said, 'you don't understand manly matters. If I turned away from what must be done, I'd be a sorry specimen of manhood.'

"Then and there, with his wife wailing and begging him to stay home and mind his business, Think-Too-Late set out for Mount Panthea.

"His journey was long and harsh. He soon ran out of what food he had taken with him; instead of fruits falling into his hands he had to scrape for roots and acorns. Nights, he shivered on the cold ground; days, he went hungry and thirsty. Nevertheless, he kept on his way. When, at last, he came to Mount Panthea, his path only grew more difficult. The higher he climbed, the sharper blew the icy gales, freezing him to the marrow. Sleet and snow blinded him, jagged rocks bloodied his hands and feet. Still, he climbed until he reached the peak.

"There, his eyes lit up as he saw a tall heap of white stones. He clawed and scrabbled away at them, and when he flung aside the last one, he cried out in both triumph and dismay. Indeed, a chest lay exposed, but hardly bigger than the palm of his hand.

" 'How can a little box hold great value?' he exclaimed. 'I've been cheated again!'

"Then he saw the coffer was sealed with the emblem of Woman-Three-Women. 'Aha,' he said to himself, 'if it belongs to her, it must be worth something, at least. Whatever it holds, I'll have it for all my pains.'

"He snatched it up. That same instant, before he could break the seal, the ground rumbled and shuddered beneath his feet. The hollow where the chest had lain gaped open. From the jaws of this pit, flames and molten rock shot upward in a crimson column reaching to the sky. The roar deafened him, the fire scorched his face. The mountain writhed and convulsed. Think-Too-Late hung on for dear life, but the mountain shrugged him off like a horse twitching away a fly. Down he tumbled, still clutching the chest, swept along on a torrent of stones and gravel.

"The earth split, a river welled up; and, next thing he knew, he was being borne farther and farther, spinning and tossing like a leaf. Behind him, a barrier of high crags jutted where once had stretched a flat plain. Springs gushed to form lakes, waterfalls poured from newly risen cliffs. Bruised and battered, Think-Too-Late was at last pitched ashore, astonished to find himself alive and his bones unbroken.

" 'That,' he said, 'was a bit more than I bargained for.'

"Picking himself up, he set about making his long way home. This journey proved easier than his first, for he taught himself to build shelters from leaves and branches, to find forage in even the roughest country; and so, when at last he trudged into his dooryard, he was not in much worse condition than when he left.

"Giving-All-Gifts ran to embrace him, weeping with joy, and in the same breath, scolding him furiously for having risked his life to gain only a little box.

" 'Better than empty-handed,' said Think-Too-Late, casting around for a means of breaking the seal, which had not yielded to any of his efforts along the way. However, no sooner had he set the chest on the ground than the lid flew open by itself.

"Giving-All-Gifts cried out and covered her face with her hands, Think-Too-Late fell back in terror as a huge black cloud swirled out of the chest. From it strode a giant figure bearing a flaming torch; and, wherever he passed, trees were blighted, fruits withered, and fields lay barren. While Think-Too-Late stared, too frozen in horror to turn away, another giant shape appeared, gripping a lash with a dozen knotted thongs; and, wherever he swung this scourge, all living things sickened, racked with plagues and pestilence. Before the cloud melted away, yet another giant sprang from it, brandishing a bloody sword; and, wherever he passed, men fought and slew each other without mercy.

"Then, as if from nowhere, crowned with a crescent moon, there stood a tall figure in a cloak shining with stars. Think-Too-Late and Giving-All-Gifts fell to their knees. Though a shimmering veil hid her face from them, they knew this was Woman-Three-Women.

" 'Think-Too-Late,' she said, in a voice that chilled his heart, 'do you know what you have done? That is what we wished to keep from you. Now you have set these monsters at large, and never again can they be called back.'

"Think-Too-Late bowed his head. 'Take my life. I pay it for the ills I unloosed.'

" 'Wretched little man,' replied Woman-Three-Women, 'do you suppose your death can make up for your deed? No. Your punishment will be far greater.'

" 'So be it,' said Think-Too-Late. 'It can be no worse than what I deserve. And yet—and yet'—here, he raised his face and a spark brightened his eyes—'despite all else, wrong or not, I did what I did. I climbed to the very top of Mount Panthea, I rode the avalanche, I was burned, frozen, nearly drowned, and lived to come back; and this, no man has ever done.'

" 'You are a fool,' said Woman-Three-Women, 'but, I

admit, you are, after a fashion, also a hero: a combination typical among mortals.'

" 'Whatever his punishment,' said Giving-All-Gifts, 'I, too, wish to suffer it with him. He is a foolish creature, as I know better than anyone; and, thus, all the more need for me to help him bear it.'

" 'So you shall,' said Woman-Three-Women, 'and give him more comfort than he merits, and show better sense than he will ever have. Now, farewell to you.'

" 'You banish us?' cried Think-Too-Late, his heart torn. 'Cast us out into some terrible wilderness? Spare my wife this fate. She has done no wrong.'

" 'You stay,' said Woman-Three-Women. 'I and the Great Ones must go from here. I have long known this would be the shape of our destinies, and a day such as this would come. It is in the grain and nature of things. You were right, Think-Too-Late. We treated you as children. As children grow up and lead their own lives, so must you.'

"Woman-Three-Women turned to Giving-All-Gifts. 'To you, I entrust the arts of planting and harvesting, of healing and consolation, and all secret knowledge you will share with all women. As for you, Think-Too-Late, your punishment is so harsh I dread to speak it. You are a hero, and you are welcome to that cold glory. But you, and all men after you, shall be forever cursed with discontent, with a spirit never at peace, curiosity never satisfied, seeking that never finds, questioning never answered. You shall be driven by a goad you sharpen yourself, and go blundering and stumbling, misjudging and misunderstanding to the end of your days. In sum, you are condemned to be human. I can inflict nothing more painful. Too much so, perhaps. Therefore, I leave you one last thing.'

"As she spoke, out of the chest flew a small white bird, so graceful and beautiful that Giving-All-Gifts caught her breath in wonder and reached out to it. And, indeed, the bird came to perch a moment on her finger before it spread its wings and fluttered away.

" 'Cherish and treat it kindly,' said Woman-Three-Women. 'It is a fragile creature, easily frightened. But, always you will find it when you need it most. Its name is Hope-Never-Lost.'

"With those words, Woman-Three-Women vanished as quickly as she had come, never to be seen again by mortal eyes."

9

The Pharmakos

And that," said Joy-in-the-Dance, folding her hands, "is how the Great Ones left us and women became keepers of wisdom, because of Think-Too-Late."

"A terrible punishment," said Fronto, with a wheezing sigh. "Being a human, let alone a poet, is difficult enough. However, compared with being an ass, I rather envy him."

Lucian had been so caught up in the girl's story, as if he himself had climbed mountains and ridden avalanches, that it took him some moments to realize he was back at the pool's side. Hoping to hear more, he asked, "Is that the end?"

"Of that story," said Joy-in-the-Dance. "After Woman-

Three-Women vanished, a mortal woman was chosen to take her place. She, and those who came after, held the title Lady of Wild Things.

"Mount Panthea and all the old sanctuaries are now places of study, where lore is handed down, as the story says, from Giving-All-Gifts. The Lady of Wild Things is first among our teachers, our guide and counselor who knows more than any of us. She teaches us to remember."

"Who needs to be taught? Everybody can remember. You just do it."

"Not the way you think. We learn by word of mouth. We memorize our lore and know it by heart. It isn't written down."

"You have all this wisdom, all these secrets," said Lucian, "and you don't even know how to write?"

"Of course we do. Mother Tongue's our first language. We certainly know how to speak it. And read it, and write it. But when it comes to lore and learning— no, Aiee-Ouch, we don't write it down. That's too dangerous.

"Don't you understand? Think about it," Joy-in-the-Dance went on. "If something's written down, it can be stolen. Or destroyed. Or copied wrong. Or changed all around so it doesn't mean what it was supposed to mean. Memory's the safest place to keep it."

"I don't see that," Lucian said. "Everything's gone forever if you happen to forget."

"We don't forget."

"That's true, my boy," put in Fronto. "It's been my experience that women never forget anything. There have been times when I wish they did."

"And all this came about because of what one man did long ago?" said Lucian.

"Not exactly," said Joy-in-the-Dance. "Once, our lore was written down. Not anymore. Not since the Bear tribe came to Arkadia. But that's a different story."

Joy-in-the-Dance closed her eyes, leaving Lucian all the more curious but none the wiser.

❧

Next day, the wolves found them.

For much of that morning, Joy-in-the-Dance led Lucian and Fronto along a smooth forest track. After a time, however, Fronto began turning skittish, uneasily sniffing the air. Lucian glimpsed ash gray streaks flickering through the brush.

"Only wolves," Joy-in-the-Dance said, unperturbed. "We're in their territory."

"Then let's get out of it," urged Fronto. "I'll be turned into meat before I'm turned into a man."

The pack broke from cover that same instant. Half a dozen of the lean, rough-coated animals stationed themselves to block the path. A huge, yellow-eyed she wolf, tongue lolling and ears laid back, loped forward.

Lucian stepped quickly ahead of Joy-in-the-Dance. He snatched up a fallen branch. The gray wolf halted and crouched. Her hackles went up and she bared her fangs. Lucian's hands shook so violently he could scarcely keep a grip on the makeshift weapon. Nevertheless, he dug in his heels and braced for her attack. The wolf fixed her eyes on him and pointed her long muzzle.

"Run, you two," Lucian ordered. "I'll hold her off."

"Don't be such an Aiee-Ouch." Joy-in-the-Dance strode next to him, pulled the branch from his hand, and tossed it aside. "She won't bite."

"What's she showing me, then? I'd call them—teeth."

"I'd show mine, too, if somebody was shaking a stick at me."

The wolf trotted up, wagging her tail. She hunkered down in front of Lucian, snuffling and nuzzling his ankles. Lucian swallowed hard. "Good doggie," he said.

"Interesting," said Joy-in-the-Dance. "She likes you. She has something in mind."

"So do I," muttered Fronto. "Galloping in the opposite direction."

"Best go with her," advised Joy-in-the-Dance as the wolf took the hem of Lucian's tunic between her teeth and tugged him toward the waiting animals.

The pack closed around him. Next thing, he was willy-nilly bounding along with them. The wolves quickened their pace, urging him on with an occasional nip at his heels. As Lucian, to his surprise, found himself able to keep up, racing faster and faster, legs at full stretch and heart pounding, he began to relish the wild excitement of it. Joy-in-the-Dance and Fronto followed well behind him.

They halted at last, where several other wolves sat on their haunches at the foot of a tall beech tree. While Fronto eyed the pack uneasily, Joy-in-the-Dance came to Lucian's side. The wolves were looking at something high above. Lucian shaded his eyes and peered upward.

There was a man at the top of the tree.

"What are you doing?" called Joy-in-the-Dance.

"Nothing," the man shouted back. "I'm stuck. I can't climb down."

"Why are you there at all?" the girl demanded. "Oh, never mind. I'll come up and get you loose."

"I'll do that," said Lucian, stepping in front of the girl. He felt marvelously sweaty after his run with the wolves, his muscles stretched and limber, and he decided that climbing a tree was exactly the challenge he wanted.

"Yes, it's man's work, of course," Joy-in-the-Dance said caustically. "I suppose you've done it a hundred times. Please, Aiee-Ouch, just keep out of the way and let me—"

"I think even a Bear man can figure it out." Calling Fronto, Lucian sprang to the poet's back and wrapped his arms around the lowest branch. He swung up and reached for one limb after the other, finding it easier than he expected.

Glancing down, however, made his head spin. The upper limbs grew thinner and bent under his weight. Swaying back and forth, trying to keep his heart from escaping by way of his mouth, he began wishing Joy-in-the-Dance had made more of an effort to keep him on the ground. Nevertheless, gritting his teeth, he clutched another branch and swung upward. What came to view was a foot, bare and mud-caked, tightly wedged in a fork of the tree.

"Good of you to stop by," said the owner of the foot. "I don't know when I'd have untangled myself, if ever. Sorry to inconvenience you."

The speaker, though a man no more than a dozen years older than Lucian, was in a terrible state of disrepair; for the most part, he was a collection of rags and tatters. Long yellow hair hung about his bruised forehead; his short beard had been plucked half away. Lucian turned his attention to the immediate matter of the foot, struggling until he pulled it free.

"Thank you. Excellent." The ragged figure set about unwinding his arms and legs. "I can manage quite well now."

The man began climbing down with surprising agility. Following his example, Lucian discovered it to be as difficult as climbing up, and far more unnerving. By accident, he adopted a quick method of reaching the ground: sliding, tumbling, bouncing off one branch after another to land sprawled in what he hoped was a triumphant posture.

"That was wonderful, Aiee-Ouch," the girl said. "I take it all back. You did perfectly, except for the one little moment when your skull hit the ground. Now, this fellow—he didn't get those stab wounds and bruises being caught up a tree."

The stranger, meantime, brushed himself off, looked around, and bobbed his head.

"Ops," he said.

"What's that?" said Lucian.

"Ops," the stranger repeated. "My name. Argeus Ops. Feel free to call me Argeus. Or Ops. Either will do. Forgive me for troubling you. I stopped to put a fledgling crow back in its nest. The parents thought I was stealing it. Understandably, they set upon me. Vigorously, too.

The little one, as it turned out, didn't need my assistance. It flew off with its parents. Then I clumsily got my foot caught. Luckily, the wolves happened along. I asked them to find help."

"You talked to them?" said Joy-in-the-Dance.

"Why, I suppose I did," said Ops. "I wonder how? Sheer necessity, no doubt. Now, how may I be of service to you? Or your donkey? He doesn't look in very good state. Is something troubling him?"

"You don't know the half of it," muttered Fronto.

"He speaks?" said Ops. "How interesting." He bowed courteously to Fronto. "No offense. I'm sure you're an excellent donkey."

"Poet," corrected Fronto. "What happened to me— never mind, I'm tired of explaining."

"As you wish." Ops turned to Lucian and Joy-in-the-Dance. "Have you two any miseries you'd like me to take on for you? Bad luck to get rid of? A loathsome disease?"

"You seem to have enough miseries of your own," said Lucian.

"It's my occupation," said Ops. "But, since I was cast out of my village, I've had little to do. I'm a pharmakos."

"Oh, no!" Joy-in-the-Dance cried in dismay. "When did this happen? Where?"

"What's a pharmakos?" asked Lucian.

"In Mother Tongue, that's the word for a scapegoat,"

said Joy-in-the-Dance. "A blame-taker. An old custom no one's followed for years. The country folk used to believe they could wish all their misfortunes onto someone else, blame him for whatever went wrong, throw him out into the wilds, and that would set everything right."

"Exactly so," said Ops. "Things went badly in my village after King Bromios made it a crime to deal with wise-women. We had no healer for ailing animals; no water-finder when two of our wells went dry; and, worst of all, no medicine woman for the infants who sickened for lack of good water. The village council decided a pharmakos could carry off their troubles. Oh, it was quite a celebration when they cast me out."

"I was afraid something like that might happen," Joy-in-the-Dance said, her eyes darkening. "They're slipping back into ways best forgotten. What next? Human sacrifice?"

"That was discussed," said Ops. "Luckily for me, they decided against it. They thought it best to lay their woes on a scapegoat.

"I'm sure they felt better, blaming me for everything," he went on, "and I was glad to do them a service. But when they got carried away, pulling my hair, hitting me with rakes and hoes—it seemed a little too much."

"No one stopped them?" demanded Joy-in-the-Dance. "No one spoke out against such a thing?"

"A few," said Ops. "Finally, most approved."

"What about the village chief?" said Joy-in-the-Dance. "He, at least, should have known better. He's supposed to have enough common sense and authority to forbid such doings."

"True," Ops agreed. "But, you see—I was the village chief."

10

Hidden Treasures

Their chief?" exclaimed Lucian. "They turned against you?"

"Not exactly," said Ops. "There's a little more to it. The treasure under the stone, for one thing. And the old shepherd. And my parents, of course."

"Please, please," Fronto put in. "Go at it a step at a time. No one can follow a tale that bolts off in all directions at once."

"Very well," said Ops. "To begin: My father-name is Argeus Ops. My mother-name is Bright-Face."

"Your parents each gave you a name?" said Lucian. "That's an unusual thing to do, isn't it?"

"I think I know why," said Joy-in-the-Dance. "In the

Bear tribe, it's the father who names his child; among my people, it's the mother."

"Yes," said Ops, "my father was a Bear man. My mother was a sanctuary maiden assigned to tend the local woods and fields."

"That's what I supposed," said Joy-in-the-Dance. Seeing a questioning look on Lucian's face, she added, "Our sanctuary maidens have always been free to marry with men of the Bear tribe or whoever they please. It doesn't happen too often these days." She turned back to Ops. "What about your parents?"

"My father died when I was a small boy; my mother, not long after," said Ops. "I was too young to remember them clearly, but the shepherd who raised me told me their story time and time again. How my father, hunting, had come upon a stag caught in a thicket. Just as he drew his bow, the most beautiful maiden he had ever seen sprang up and flung her arms around the stag's neck. She warned him if he tried to kill the creature he would have to kill her first.

"Naturally, he let the stag go free. He and the maiden fell in love at first sight. They dwelt happily together in the forest, and he never hunted again.

"When my mother knew that her life-thread had spun to its end, she gave me into the care of an old shepherd and his wife. They fostered and raised me as lovingly as if I had been their own. I helped tend the sheep and do other little tasks.

"When I was old enough to understand, the couple told me that my parents had hidden my birthright under a certain stone. The shepherd led me to a glade near the pasture and pointed out a boulder taller than I was. I begged him to move it for me so that I might possess what was underneath.

" 'That is forbidden to me,' he said. 'Your dear mother told me that only when you yourself move the stone shall you have what lies below.'

"Impatiently, I tried to wrestle it loose. But, of course, I was too small and weak. Even so, time after time, I would go and test my strength against it. Through each passing year, I struggled to raise the boulder, always failing. Often, I would sit on it, playing my shepherd's pipe, dreaming of what could have been treasured up for me, while the sheep, gently bleating—"

"Oh, get on with it!" cried Fronto. "No need to string it out, we understand the situation. There, Lucian, is an example of bad storytelling. Ops, for the sake of mercy and my patience, come to the point."

"Oh—yes, well, after I reached the strength of young manhood, a day arrived when I did shift the stone a little. I sweated and strained, and at last I rolled it away. Under it, I found a pair of sandals and a silver amulet and chain. Puzzled as much as excited, I picked them up and ran to the cottage.

"Instead of joy and pride at my accomplishment, the shepherd and his wife gazed at me with sadness.

" 'Alas, the day has come when you must leave us,' the shepherd said. 'The amulet is for your protection; the sandals for you to walk your own road. When the sandals wear out, there will you stop and stay.'

"They hung the amulet around my neck and put the sandals on my feet. With loving farewells, I set out from the cottage. My sandals were stout and well crafted; but, in time, the bindings broke, the soles came loose. Just as they fell from my feet, I found myself nearing a small village. I entered it, though hardly believing I would wish to stay there.

"The folk heartily welcomed me and showed me all the hospitality due a stranger—less than they would have liked, for their provisions were scant. The reason, they told me, was the constant raiding of their stores and granaries.

"A band of wanderers prowled the fringes of the village, darting in to pilfer whatever came to hand. 'Worse than mice,' one man complained, 'and too quick to catch.' 'A nuisance growing into a pest into a plague,' another added, 'gnawing away a little here, a little there.

If it keeps on, there won't be enough for us; or them, either.'

"The villagers had found no way to stop this raiding. As I listened, a plan took shape in my mind. I offered to help them, warning them to do as I instructed, without question. At their wits' end, they eagerly agreed.

"Next, I went alone to where this rootless band crouched in their makeshift camp. A ragtag lot of starvelings they were; men, women, and children, unkempt, round-eyed with hunger, for even what they stole was barely enough to serve them.

" 'Friends,' I declared, 'why waste your time and strength being sneak thieves? Walk with me straight into the village. You shall have all you ask and more.' However, I insisted on their following my orders and doing whatever I required.

"That they vowed and followed me—to the dismay of the villagers, who nevertheless kept silent, as they had promised.

" 'Take what you please,' I told the wretched band, pointing to the granaries. 'Take all, if that suits you. But—the grain must be threshed and winnowed first, and you must lend a hand in doing it.'

"Scowling, glaring, villagers and strangers nevertheless joined in the work. I kept them so busy they forgot to distrust one another, and there was even some good-natured jesting back and forth. That night, I called for a festival with dancing on the threshing room floor; and there, high spirits and laughter softened hard feelings.

" 'Before the grain is shared out,' I now told them, 'part must be set aside for the animals and for brewing, and the rest ground into flour. This is a long, hard task, so all must join in.'

"For days, the strangers labored at grinding the grain, receiving food enough to satisfy their hunger. When they finished, I declared, 'This is well and good, but the flour must be baked into bread. You must help to knead and shape the loaves before you claim anything more.'

"And so it went," Ops continued, "one common task after another until planting season came round and I required the wanderers to help in plowing and sowing. By this time, they were no longer wanderers. They had found occupations among the villagers, some were even betrothed or married, with little ones on the way, and few remembered when there had been ill will.

"I was chosen by all to be village chieftain and leader of the council. It was then, at last, I told the former strangers they were free, if they chose, to take everything they wanted and depart.

" 'Go from here?' retorted a lad who had apprenticed himself to a potter. 'Live hand-to-mouth in the woods? I'm no such fool.'

" 'We can't spare them,' added the winemaker. 'How did we get along without them? Here they all stay, as friends and kindred.'

"The village prospered," said Ops, "until, as I told you, we were forbidden to deal with wise-women. As things turned worse, the villagers grew desperate. Their fearful thoughts went back to a grim and ancient custom. They demanded a scapegoat.

"By no amount of reasoning, pleading, or angry protest could I change their minds. The council, among themselves, had already settled on the victim: an old woman, half-blind and so feeble she could barely put one foot in front of the other. 'Who better?' they declared. 'Her life-thread is at its end. As she is no use to herself, she can be of use to our village.'

"This I straightway refused. 'If she is so close to death, she will have no strength to carry the burden of blame.'

"They passed over the old woman but next chose a poor, half-witted boy. 'What difference can it make to him?' they said. 'His brain is addled, he will neither know nor care what becomes of him.'

"Again, I refused. 'Your victim must accept his fate of his own will and full understanding. Otherwise, as well sacrifice a dumb beast or a lump of clay.'

" 'You have only one choice,' I told them. 'I am your pharmakos.'

"They shouted against this, protesting that I had saved their village, guided them wisely, and they honored and valued me above all others.

" 'All the more reason,' I answered. 'A sacrifice that costs nothing is no sacrifice. Accept me or no one.'

"I confess I hoped this would bring them to their senses, but their desperation was too great. So, I became their scapegoat.

"And that," Ops concluded, "is how it came about. They drove me from the village, pursued me into the woods, where I outdistanced them. You know the rest."

"What a story!" exclaimed Lucian. "But it's not a tale, it happened to you. It's your own life."

"Very touching," admitted Fronto. "But, Ops, if you tell it again, go at it more briskly. Forget that business about tootling on your pipe and sheep bleating. Who cares? Now, as for my own story—"

"I want to know about the amulet," Joy-in-the-Dance broke in. "Ops, what became of it?"

"I still have it." Ops dipped into the wreckage of his shirt and fished out a silver disk at the end of a chain. The girl nodded in recognition. Lucian, peering over her shoulder, saw the figures of three women clasping hands.

"This means your mother put you under the protection of the Lady of Wild Things," said Joy-in-the-Dance. "Which also means, at the moment, you're under my protection. Fronto, you explain it to him. I want a word with Aiee-Ouch."

"My account won't take as long as his," said Fronto. "Then, Ops, my good fellow, perhaps you'd like a chance to provide your scapegoat services? I have a number of personal complaints and grievances from long before I was given my present shape. I'll be happy to lay them on you."

"I'd appreciate that," said Ops.

Leaving the wolves sitting in a circle around Fronto and Ops, Joy-in-the-Dance drew Lucian apart. She glanced back toward the pharmakos. "He'll have to come with us. He's entitled to the Lady's protection and I'll see that he gets it.

"Another thing—" She paused, looking away for some moments. Then, turning her eyes squarely on him, she added, with much effort, "Thank you for defending me against the wolves."

"Oh, yes, those ferocious wolves," retorted Lucian. "Those slavering jaws and sharp teeth, ready to tear you to pieces. All I did was make a fool of myself. You knew perfectly well they were friendly."

"But you didn't know it," said Joy-in-the-Dance. "So, thank you."

The unemployed scapegoat was delighted to accompany them. The wolves, reaching the limit of their territory, vanished as quickly and silently as they had appeared. The forest had begun to thin out, Lucian glimpsed high crags in the distance, and Joy-in-the-Dance headed straight toward them. With Ops in tow, however, progress was not as rapid. He continually halted for one reason or another. If he found a beetle struggling on its back, he would stop to set it on its legs. Crossing a stream, he noticed a beaver lodge in disrepair and insisted on delaying long enough for him to gather twigs to mend it.

To Lucian's surprise, and without his asking, Joy-in-the-Dance began pointing out patterns of stars as they rose glittering in the evening sky. He watched and listened, fascinated, as she explained how to find directions and calculate time.

"I didn't think you were supposed to tell men about such things," Lucian said.

"I've been wondering if you were right about sharing our secrets. Well, it won't do any harm to share these. They aren't the truly big mysteries. Those, you men couldn't even begin to understand."

"You've never taken the chance to find out."

"And, dear Aiee-Ouch, we don't intend to."

"My name's Lucian. I told you that when we first met. For somebody who remembers everything, you seem to keep forgetting it."

"Don't be surly. You aren't good at it," said Joy-in-the-Dance. "As for when we first met"—she gave him a sidelong smile—"I haven't forgotten."

In addition to star patterns, the girl willingly pointed out plants he never would have noticed—fever-begone, wound-balm, quicken-the-heart—as she named them and explained their use. In the course of the days, she was obliged, with some reluctance, to admit that he had grown clever enough to find these herbs without her guidance.

In his eagerness to collect the best medicinal plants, Lucian took to roaming farther afield on his own. One afternoon, outdistancing Joy-in-the-Dance, he clambered up through the scrub-covered foothills. He halted, his eyes wide in amazement as he looked down into a green cup of pastureland. The rarest and most valuable of herbs, wound-balm, covered the lower slope in unbelievable abundance.

Excitedly calling Joy-in-the-Dance to see what he had discovered, he scrambled down. Almost at the bottom, he heard something buzz past his ear. A stone rattled into the undergrowth, then another.

Warning the girl to stay away, Lucian hastily turned back toward the crest. That same instant, a hard object connected with his skull and he lost interest in the outside world.

11

Catch-a-Tick

"T here must be something about your head," Joy-in-
the-Dance remarked, "that makes people want to
hit it."

The girl, sitting on the floor beside him, held an
earthen bowl of some sharp-smelling concoction. Fronto
was there; and Ops, smiling in relief. As best Lucian
could judge, he was on a straw pallet in a chamber
domed like a beehive. Shaggy figures with dark, leathery
faces peered down curiously. Stubby horns jutted from
their brows, curly beards covered their chins.

"Goats?" Lucian blinked and looked again. They
were, he realized, men in goatskin jackets. Their horns
were twisted locks of hair stiffened with clay. He started
up. "Who—or what are they?"

"Gently, gently," Joy-in-the-Dance whispered. "Don't worry. They're friends."

Exploring the landscape of his head, Lucian discovered a lump the size of a goose egg behind his ear. "What do you call this?" he muttered. "A token of goodwill?"

"Awake, are you?" boomed a voice. "By the beard of the Great Goat, it's about time."

The speaker was bandy-legged, stocky, with grizzled hair falling in ringlets around his pointed ears. His disposition struck Lucian as being as rough as his garments.

"Buckthorn Goat King," Joy-in-the-Dance said under her breath. "I've told him all about us. He can be helpful—if he wants to."

"Here's the little wretch who cracked your noggin," declared Buckthorn. He kept a tight grip on the ear of a snub-nosed boy dressed like his elders but with a stumpier set of clay horns. "Catch-a-Tick. I could call him a few other names, too. He's had a good hiding. Yes, and by the Great Goat's left hind foot, it's one he won't forget."

So saying, Buckthorn shoved Catch-a-Tick in front of Lucian. The boy dropped to his knees. Despite the humble posture, his bright, black eyes stared boldly and a grin played around his lips.

"I was punished for missing you," said Catch-a-Tick,

"not for hitting you. We Goat Folk are supposed to hit our target with the first shot."

Being ambushed and brought down by a small boy did not raise Lucian's self-esteem; especially as he had, once again, looked like a fool in the eyes of Joy-in-the-Dance. He frowned sternly. Catch-a-Tick, in trying to keep himself from laughing, seemed so close to bursting, choking, and making such faces that Lucian finally chuckled despite himself. "All right, kidling. No hard feelings except for the lump you gave me. If you've had the tanning you deserve, that's the end of it."

"Oh, no, it isn't," said Buckthorn. "He's here for the rest of his punishment. He broke a sacred law of the Goat Folk. You came unarmed, a stranger. We owe you hospitality, not a crack on the noggin."

"I only wanted to test my new sling," protested Catch-a-Tick. He held up a leather pouch dangling from rawhide thongs.

"Hold your tongue," cried Buckthorn. "You know our law." He turned to Lucian. "He's in your hands. Do whatever you want with him." Buckthorn hesitated a moment, then went on firmly. "By rule, if you choose, you can claim his life."

The chamber was silent, the onlookers held their breath. Catch-a-Tick's grin faded.

"His life? For a knock on the head?" replied Lucian. "Surely not. Let him go. That's that, over and done with."

The watching Goat Folk breathed again. Buckthorn, though clearly relieved, held up a gnarled hand. "Not done with. Demand something of him, no matter what. That's our law. We obey it. So will you."

"There's nothing I want from him."

"You think of something." Buckthorn glowered. "Speak out now, or it won't sit well with me or any Goat Folk."

Lucian pondered for a few moments then folded his arms and addressed Catch-a-Tick.

"I won't claim your life. I already have one of my own and trouble enough with it. However, you don't look very repentant. In fact, I've never seen anybody who looked less repentant. I intend, therefore, to pronounce a harsh sentence on you. I condemn you—to teach me how to use that sling."

"Acceptable!" Buckthorn clapped his hands. "Honorably judged, by the horns of the Great Goat! His mother will be glad you let him off so easily. She dotes on him." The king's face softened. "So do I, for that matter. The little goat-scut is my son."

Catch-a-Tick winked. "Next time, I'll aim better."

"Please," said Lucian, "don't."

For a king, Buckthorn's house was modest. Though somewhat roomier than the other dozen or so dwellings, it had the same beehive shape, a hole in its dome that vented smoke from the fire pit, and, like the rest, it was built close against the hillside. Goats and chickens wandered in as they pleased. May-Apple, plump wife of Buckthorn, bustled about, stuffing goat cheese into Lucian's mouth, pouring goat's milk down his throat, adding fresh straw to his pallet, and every way showing gratitude for his dealing so kindly with the irrepressible Catch-a-Tick.

Buckthorn, also pleased by Lucian's judgment, had agreed to help them all he could. He and a few of his kinsmen had gone with Joy-in-the-Dance to see the state of the mountain passes; for she intended crossing the barrier of snowy crags and reaching the grasslands beyond.

To Lucian's surprise and discomfort, the girl's absence made him feel as if he had a toothache in his chest. Since Fronto was absorbed in long talks with Ops, and Lucian was too restless to sit waiting for her to come back, he decided this was the best moment to execute his sentence on Catch-a-Tick.

"You Goat Folk live very nicely here," said Lucian as the boy led him through the pasture. "Snug and peaceful," he added, half wistfully. "The goats should be pleasant company."

"They don't do much of anything. It gets boring after a while," said Catch-a-Tick, with a shrug. He stopped beside a stream and knelt to collect a handful of smooth stones. "Here, watch this."

He set a pebble into the leather pouch. Then he whirled the sling over his head, let loose a thong, and the missile shot across the pasture. "Your turn, now."

Lucian, taking the sling, followed the boy's example. Instead of flying straight, the pebble nearly hit his own ear. Catch-a-Tick burst out laughing, rolling about on the grass and kicking his heels in the air.

"Do you want me to brain myself?" cried Lucian. "I think I'll claim your life, after all. I'll have you boiled in your own sauce."

Chuckling, Catch-a-Tick repeated his demonstration and Lucian began again. It took half the morning, but at last he caught the knack and could send a stone almost as far as his teacher and hit his target more often than not.

Delighted with himself, Lucian squatted by the edge of the stream and splashed water on his face. Next moment, sputtering and flapping his arms, he was boosted head over heels into the current. If he had envied a herd boy's peaceful life among the goats, that prospect vanished as he glimpsed a burly, long-bearded billy goat observing him with wicked amusement. Catch-a-Tick, capering on the bank, looked enormously entertained.

"Stand up on those long legs of yours," called the boy. "It isn't deep. Climb out."

Despite this advice, Lucian could not keep his feet from slipping. Catch-a-Tick shrugged out of his jacket and dove into the water. He set Lucian upright, then paddled around him, cavorting like an otter.

"Can't you swim?" The boy bobbed up and down. "Look—take a breath. You won't sink. Move your arms, kick your heels."

Lucian awkwardly imitated Catch-a-Tick and, to his astonishment, found himself actually moving across the surface. At the boy's urging, he soon dared to swim underwater. Suddenly, he was in a world where fish darted through the water like birds through the air; and Lucian himself soared up and down as if weightless, skimming over the greenery rising from the stream bed. Reveling in his new skill, he bobbed up only long enough to fill his lungs, then plunged down again. For the rest of the afternoon, he divided his time between slinging stones and jumping in and out of the stream.

"Catch-a-Tick," said Lucian as they rested on the bank, "you're a good fellow. I won't have you boiled."

"You're not a bad sort, either," said the boy, chewing a blade of grass. "For an outlander. My father says you came all the way from Metara. It must be a great city."

"It is. They say the port alone is a city in itself. Docks, taverns, ships with masts as tall as trees and sails big enough to cover this pasture. The palace, where I lived. The public square, the shops, eating houses—"

Catch-a-Tick whistled. "You've seen all that?"

"Just some of it, passing through. Fronto and I had to get out as fast as we could. Otherwise, a couple of thieving soothsayers would have chopped me to bits."

"Marvelous!" burst out Catch-a-Tick.

"With huge meat cleavers—" A glint came to Lucian's eyes; then he glanced over his shoulder, as if Joy-in-the-Dance were listening from somewhere. "Ah—not exactly. But it was a narrow escape."

"Then what?" demanded Catch-a-Tick.

"Not much. We came up against a troop of warriors, but—"

"You call that not much? Did you fight them hand to hand? Did you have a sword?"

"A sword was definitely involved," said Lucian. "Then Fronto got stolen, I had to risk my neck getting him back. After that, we fell in with a pack of wolves—"

"And they made you leader of the pack?"

"Well—I did run with them awhile," said Lucian. "That was before I rescued Ops from the highest tree I'd ever seen."

Catch-a-Tick's eyes lit up with awe and admiration.
"Then?"

"Nothing, really. Until you cracked my skull with a
rock." However, as Catch-a-Tick insisted, Lucian went
over his account again, warming to his tale as Catch-a-
Tick excitedly urged him on. By the time he finished
telling and retelling, Lucian was uncertain what was fact
and what was preposterous invention; and he was glad
that Joy-in-the-Dance, at the moment, was elsewhere.
Dusk had gathered when they returned to the beehive
palace, Catch-a-Tick still demanding more.

Lucian's face was red and smarting from sunburn and
his arms ached. When May-Apple scolded the boy for
tiring their guest, Catch-a-Tick waved away her reproach.
"He's not tired, he's a hero. You should have heard. They
tried to chop him up with meat cleavers. He fought an
army of warriors single-handedly. He led a pack of
wolves—"

"Great Goat!" cried May-Apple, throwing up her
hands. "And him only a lad!"

"Nothing out of the ordinary," said Lucian, with the
modesty he thought befitting a hero. "Anyone would
have done the same."

12

The Great Goat
and Never-Filled

Joy-in-the-Dance, Buckthorn, and the others came back that evening. They had found the nearest passes blocked by deep snow and rockfalls. "Buckthorn knows another way, a couple of days east of here," the girl told Lucian, shucking off her borrowed goatskin cape and leggings. "He'll guide us. It should be open enough to get through. We'll start at first light tomorrow—your nose is blistered, Aiee-Ouch—so, best get a good night's sleep."

"Why does she call you Aiee-Ouch?" Catch-a-Tick asked Lucian. "It's a silly name for a hero."

"Because—well, because she does," said Lucian.

Catch-a-Tick nodded sagely. "She's a girl, and who knows why they do anything. I still think it's silly."

"So do I," said Lucian. To his own surprise, he added, "But I'm getting to like it."

May-Apple had found capes and leggings for Lucian and Ops, as well as for Joy-in-the-Dance. In the dawn chill, they gratefully put on these garments. Fronto, eager to start, hardly complained at all about being laden with provisions. Catch-a-Tick, however, complained loudly and lengthily, pleading, cajoling, and demanding to be taken along. Buckthorn seemed tempted to let the boy have his way, but May-Apple would hear none of it. So, as the journeyers made ready to leave, the downcast Catch-a-Tick went to Lucian.

"Here." The boy held out his sling. "For you."

"But that's your best one," said Lucian. "It's too valuable to give away."

"You might need it," said Catch-a-Tick, pressing it into Lucian's hands. "This, too," he added, offering a pouch full of smooth stones. He wiped his nose on his sleeve, then regained his usual grin. "Good-bye—Aiee-Ouch."

"Good-bye, kidling," said Lucian, before hurrying to join the impatient Fronto. "Next time, we'll see who hits who."

That day, and most of the following, Buckthorn led them along the lower, gentler slopes. As they drew closer to the high pass, the Goat King, with a couple of his kinsmen bringing up the rear, nimbly picked his way over steeper and rougher trails. Lucian was glad for his warm cape; the air had turned crisp, sharply scented with pine and fir. These mountains, Joy-in-the-Dance told him, were part of the range that sprang up when Think-Too-Late had been swept from the crest of Mount Panthea. "Or so," she added, "that's how the story goes."

"Well, now," put in Buckthorn, overhearing the girl's comment, "if that's what you've heard—no, those crags were here long before any such tale. They're from the time of the Great Goat himself. Just as we've been here long before Woman-Three-Women and anyone else."

"Your people were first in Arkadia?" said Lucian, his curiosity, as always, aroused.

"Born and bred in these very hills," said Buckthorn. "Until then, there was nobody here at all."

"My dear Buckthorn," said Fronto, who had been listening to this exchange, "I wouldn't dream of denying that your ancestors are as ancient as any in the country, but they had to come from somewhere to get here in the first place."

"No, they didn't," declared Buckthorn. "As for lowlanders, bog trotters, you citified folk, and such, all you lot are newcomers compared with us." The Goat King, during this, had taken a couple of stones from his jacket.

Lucian watched, fascinated, as Buckthorn struck one against the other. Sparks flew to the dry moss and twigs that one of Buckthorn's fellows had gathered in a pile; up sprang a flame, which the Goat King fed with larger branches until a good-size fire blazed and crackled.

"I'd like to hear more about that," said Lucian.

"I can only tell you what's been told to me," said Buckthorn, squatting on his heels while the other Goat Folk drifted over to join him. "So, one day, as it happened, the Great Goat was out and about, walking in his pasture—"

"One moment," broke in Fronto. "As a poet, I don't like to niggle and nitpick over small details. But for the sake of accuracy, when you say 'walking,' was he strolling around on his hind legs? Or all fours? In which case, you might have said 'trotting.'"

"By a billy goat's beard, it makes no difference," retorted Buckthorn. "He could do anything he pleased. He was walking. Or trotting. Or both."

"Were there other animals in those days?" Lucian ventured to ask.

"Of course," Buckthorn answered. "They were here before anybody, but that's naught to do with this tale. Now, as I'm trying to tell you, one day the Great Goat was out and about, walking in his pasture, when he came to the edge of a pond. And there sat a little creature with a bald head big and round as a pumpkin, a mouth like a frog's, a pair of skinny arms and legs, and eyes googling and goggling in two directions at the same time.

" 'Good morning,' said the Great Goat. 'I haven't had the pleasure of meeting you.'

" 'I live at the bottom of this pond,' said the creature, 'and eat whatever bits and pieces come my way. But these are lean days and I'm perishing with hunger.'

" 'I'll see what I can do about that,' said the Great Goat, taking pity on the creature, who was sighing and groaning and holding his empty little belly. So the Great Goat led him to his house and sat him down at the table.

"Then the Great Goat brought out a wheel of cheese and cut a wedge from it. Instead of the wedge, the creature took hold of the wheel and swallowed it down in one gulp.

" 'You've an appetite bigger than yourself,' said the Great Goat, 'and the inside of your paunch must be larger than the outside.'

"The Great Goat then cut a slice from a loaf of bread; but the creature gobbled up the loaf instead of the slice; and, instead of the cup of milk that the Great Goat set out for him, he poured the whole pitcherful down his gullet. Then he licked clean all the jars of honey, ate all the sacks of wheat and barley, chomped up all the stores of fruit and vegetables, and looked around for more. Yet his belly was shrunken as ever, despite what he had crammed into it.

" 'My name is Never-Filled!' the creature cried in a terrible voice. 'I've eaten everything in your house, now I'll eat you, horns, hooves, and all. After that, I'll eat up the whole world.'

" 'An ambitious undertaking,' said the Great Goat, who understood that he had to deal with something more than a feeble, googly-eyed pond creature, 'but I think not.'

"And so, when Never-Filled opened a mouth gaping like a cavern and sprang at him, the Great Goat changed himself into a grain of wheat and hid in a crack in the floor."

"Amazing!" Lucian said aside to Fronto. "Who'd have ever expected anything like that?"

"A slight weakness in storytelling," said Fronto. "Buckthorn should have hinted right at the start that the Great Goat had such a power. This way, it comes at you all of a sudden. But, I suppose you might accept it as an element of surprise. Yet, if I were doing it—"

"Hush, you two," whispered Joy-in-the-Dance. "Let Buckthorn tell it his own way."

"I already said the Great Goat could do anything he

pleased." Buckthorn cocked a severe eye at Fronto. "And you might notice that of all the things he could have chosen, he didn't turn himself into a jackass.

"Now, where was I? Yes, he turned himself into a grain of wheat, but Never-Filled turned into a hen, scratched him out of the crack, and swallowed him down.

"But the Great Goat turned into an egg, and when the hen laid that egg, out hatched the Great Goat as a fuzzy little chick and scurried away.

"But Never-Filled turned into a weasel and darted to snap him up. Then the Great Goat jumped into the pond and became a fish; and Never-Filled changed into an otter and swam to seize him. Then the Great Goat changed into a bird and flew off; but Never-Filled changed into a hawk, with wings so wide they made the sky dark as night.

" 'A good trick,' the Great Goat said to himself, 'but I have a few of my own.'

"The Great Goat turned himself into a mountain valley, but Never-Filled turned into a rainstorm and flooded it. Then the Great Goat turned into a rainbow; but Never-Filled turned into a north wind and blew it away.

" 'This is beginning to get serious,' said the Great Goat and turned into a summer day; but Never-Filled turned into a winter night and snowed all over him.

" 'I need a little more elbow room,' said the Great Goat, and he turned into the full moon; but Never-Filled turned into a giant rat and began gnawing it.

" 'Enough toying with him,' said the Great Goat. 'Now I'll have the game go my way.'

"And so, just when Never-Filled had gnawed the moon down to a sliver, the Great Goat turned into a comet and circled around so fast that he flew behind the giant rat and set his tail on fire. Squeaking and squealing, Never-Filled shot across the sky; and now things were the other way round, for it was the Great Goat who went chasing after him.

"They streaked through the sky, through all four houses of the seasons, until Never-Filled spied a black hole and darted into it. 'Let him dare come out,' said the Great Goat, 'and I'll be waiting to give him a good butt in his ratty rear end.'

"The Great Goat's been standing guard, protecting us ever since," Buckthorn said, pointing at the night sky. "There, you can see him. Those stars—they're his horns; those others, his legs; and those three little ones, his beard."

"That's very interesting," said Joy-in-the-Dance. "We call those stars Amaltheia, 'Tender Nurse,' but she's a nanny goat, not a billy goat."

"Ah, well, I'm afraid you women have it wrong way

round," said Buckthorn. "It's a billy goat, no question."

Joy-in-the-Dance smiled knowingly. "You men like to think so."

"But, Buckthorn," Lucian put in, "you were going to tell about the Goat Folk."

"So I was," Buckthorn said. "Yes, what happened, you see, was this: While the Great Goat was running after Never-Filled, he kicked loose a herd of stars. They fell on these very mountains so hard they buried themselves into the ground; but then they sprouted up as men and women—us, the Goat Folk."

"Come now, Buckthorn," said Fronto, "do you mean to tell us your ancestors grew out of the ground—like so many cabbages?"

"We're here, aren't we?" said Buckthorn. "That's proof enough. And I don't take kindly to having my ancestors likened to cabbages." He went back to poking the fire.

"A wild tale," Lucian said later to Fronto. "I don't know what to make of it."

"A bit rough in spots, but it does have its moments," said Fronto. "A professional storyteller should be able to polish it up."

Lucian's last glimpse, before he shut his eyes to sleep, was of Buckthorn sitting by the fire. In the flickering light, he looked half-man, half-goat, and ancient as the hills themselves. As Lucian's dreams went spinning in his head, he saw Buckthorn as the Great Goat, with Joy-in-the-Dance riding on his back across an ocean of stars, her shining hair streaming like a comet's tail as she vanished behind the moon; and Never-Filled had turned into a dragon, snapping its jaws so ferociously that its teeth came loose and fell to earth; and there was Catch-a-Tick, May-Apple, and the Goat Folk popping up where the dragon's teeth had fallen; while Lucian swam through the stars as fast as he could after Joy-in-the-Dance.

She was nudging him. Still dream-fuddled, Lucian blinked at her. "I found you, after all."

"Aiee-Ouch, what in the world are you mumbling about?" said Joy-in-the-Dance. "I've been here all the time."

13

Lord See-Far-Ahead

Buckthorn's judgment proved to be right. As he expected, the pass was clear, with only a few stretches of snow, and there the journeyers took leave of their guides.

"Here, lad," said Buckthorn, handing Lucian a pair of firestones. "You may have use for them. And you, little pythoness, your way should be easy now." After clasping hands with Ops, he gave Fronto a good-natured whack on the rump. "Poet, I forgive you for talking about my ancestors as if they were cabbages. I hope you'll soon be walking on two legs instead of four."

They soon gained the rolling plains beyond the pass. Lucian had never imagined such a sea of green, where grass often reached higher than his waist. It shimmered and rippled in the sunlight, and he plunged through it as if he were swimming. Joy-in-the-Dance, pressing ahead of him, constantly scanned the crests and ridges.

"There—yes, there they are." She pointed to the high ground rising just ahead. "I knew they'd find us."

Across the brow of the hill, a loose string of a dozen mounted figures had suddenly sprung up. It could have been the dazzling sunlight, or his eyes playing tricks on him; but, for a moment, Lucian thought they were half-horse, half-human. They sat their steeds so closely they seemed to grow from the forequarters of their animals. They bore long, slender lances topped with horsetail streamers; short, oddly curved bows and quivers of arrows were slung about their backs. Sighting Joy-in-the-Dance, they sped down the slope.

As they galloped closer, Lucian saw them to be men and women dressed alike in fringed tunics and trousers of soft leather, yellow hair tumbling below their shoulders, their faces sunburnt to dark gold, cheeks and brows painted with bands of crimson and white streaks of gypsum.

Before Lucian knew what was happening to him, one of the riders bore down at full tilt. Hardly slowing his gait, he leaned over to seize Lucian by the jacket, hauled him up in one powerful motion, and set him in front of himself. The bewildered Lucian groped for reins or harness, but there were none. So he could only wrap his arms around the horse's neck and cling for dear life as the rider wheeled and galloped after his companions.

What had become of Ops, Lucian had no idea; but he glimpsed Fronto being swept along amid the horsemen. Joy-in-the-Dance was out of sight. After that, Lucian gave all his attention to hanging on as best he could while horse and rider flew over the ground without seeming to touch it.

At last, they halted at a circle of bell-shaped tents of horsehide, lashed with leather thongs. Here, the rider sprang down easily, and though he spoke in a language Lucian could not understand, Lucian was clearly being ordered to dismount—which he did by more or less falling off the steed's back.

Joy-in-the-Dance had already jumped down. By the time Lucian picked himself up, she had run to a tall man who had come out of the largest tent and flung herself into his outstretched arms.

Ops slid off his own mount and went to fetch Fronto from the midst of the horses. Wheezing, puffing, rolling his eyes, the poet muttered to Lucian, "They galloped me so fast I thought I'd sprout wings at any moment. Yes, and a couple of the mares took quite a fancy to me. I tried to explain my condition, but they didn't understand a word I said."

Joy-in-the-Dance was beckoning urgently. Lucian, still collecting his wits, elbowed through the crowd gathering at the tent.

"Hurry along, Aiee-Ouch," Joy-in-the-Dance called. "And you, Ops. Fronto, you needn't worry; I've told about your difficulty. Here, Aiee-Ouch, this is the *basileus*—oh, I'm sorry, I forgot you don't speak Mother Tongue—chieftain of the Horse Clan, Lord See-Far-Ahead."

The man so named stood head and shoulders taller than Lucian. A thin circlet of gold held a long mane of tawny, gray-streaked hair; a sun disk of beaten gold hung at his throat. His craggy face had been sunburnt to the same color as his leather garments, bands of yellow ochre and white gypsum barred his high cheekbones and arching bridge of his nose. For a moment, he looked Lucian up and down through lightning-blue eyes, then nodded with an air of easy authority and amused tolerance. Lucian shifted uncomfortably, suspecting that Lord See-Far-Ahead was perfectly capable of taking him apart limb from limb if he had any interest in doing so.

"*Khaire*. Hail and greetings." The chieftain, in a flowing gesture, raised one hand palm outward and laid the other on his heart. "Aiee-Ouch? What tribe is that?"

"Not a tribe, it's just what I call him," put in Joy-in-the-Dance. "He's Lucian."

"Why, then, do you call him by a name not his own?" See-Far-Ahead raised an eyebrow. "What is its meaning? Surely, it has one. All things have meaning."

The girl did not answer. For some reason, to Lucian's surprise, she actually blushed. The chieftain continued, "Be welcome, Lucian Aiee-Ouch. And you, little *parthenope*, it gladdens my heart to see you. I am told you are a pythoness in Arkadia Beyond-the-Mountains. A high honor, Terpsichore, but one that keeps you too long apart from us."

"Terpsichore?" Lucian whispered to her as the chieftain turned his gaze on Fronto and Ops.

"My clan name, that's all."

"Are these people your kindred?"

"Yes, but I'm only partly of the Horse Clan," said Joy-in-the-Dance. "See-Far-Ahead's my father. My mother— well, my mother's the Lady of Wild Things."

14

Yellow-Mane and Cloud-Rising

Lucian stared at the girl as if he had never seen her before. "And you said nothing?" he burst out. "Nothing? All this time?"

"It was better you didn't know. I was wrong even telling you I was the pythoness. I certainly wasn't going to tell you who my mother is."

"Why? Another secret you kept to yourself? Because you couldn't trust a Bear man? Is that it? Because you were afraid—"

"Yes, I was afraid." The girl's chin shot up. "Suppose we'd been caught. They'd have made you tell everything you knew about me, they'd have beaten it out of you. Bromios would have won more than he hoped: the pythoness—and the Lady's daughter, as well."

"I don't believe that. You were never afraid we'd be caught."

"Yes, I was," Joy-in-the-Dance said in a low voice. "More than I let on. And something else." She paused a long moment, then added, all in one breath, "I didn't tell you because I didn't want you to think of me as anyone's daughter, no matter whose. Only as me. As I am."

"How could I, when I never knew who you were in the first place? I don't understand what you're talking about."

"Of course you don't." She turned and strode from the tent, joining the maidens beckoning to her.

"Let be." See-Far-Ahead put a hand on Lucian's shoulder as he was about to follow. "She has given you something of value: the truth in her heart."

"Oh?" Lucian said angrily. "How do I know that?"

"You have yet to learn the ways of women." See-Far-Ahead smiled at him. "It is an endless study."

⋘

That evening, See-Far-Ahead ordered a feast, with music and dancing. The sides of the tent had been unlaced to make a sort of pavilion. Still angry and confused, Lucian sat silently with Ops and Fronto, who the chieftain chose to rank as a poet and only a temporary jackass.

Lucian had seen nothing of Joy-in-the-Dance until

See-Far-Ahead signaled the Dance of Colts to begin. Then he caught sight of her among the young men and women forming a ring around a blazing fire. Like the other maidens, she was now ceremonially dressed in a long, fringed skirt, with beads, bracelets, and flat slippers bound with colored ribbons, her hair in one thick braid.

"I'd be tempted to try a few steps," said Fronto, "if I had two feet instead of four. No matter, I'll investigate this basin of—what is it? Fermented mare's milk? A delightfully heady brew."

As the musicians plucked stringed instruments, tapped drums, and shook rods fitted with jingling metal disks, the dancers joined, broke away, and joined again. Laughing and smiling, her head flung back, her arms shaping graceful movements, the girl sprang lightly in and out of the swirling patterns. Lucian preferred to ignore the glances cast on her by the tall, loose-limbed youths of the camp.

"She dances well," said See-Far-Ahead. "Her feet tread the measure, but I think her heart turns toward you. And what of yours, young man with a name not his own?"

Lucian did not answer. See-Far-Ahead gave him a look half-warning, half-pitying, and did not pursue the question.

Joy-in-the-Dance, cheeks flushed and eyes shining,

came back to the tent with a handsome young warrior, Swift-Arrow, the chieftain's second in command. He was the rider who, earlier, had so easily snatched up Lucian, who now felt singularly ungrateful.

See-Far-Ahead clapped his hands and summoned the *lyrikos*, a bent-backed elder with white hair falling below his shoulders. The chieftain addressed him most respectfully, inviting him to entertain the guests with song or story.

Fronto raised his nose from the basin. "What did See-Far-Ahead call him?" he asked Lucian. "Gold-Horse? Something equine, whatever. I've heard of these minstrels. They're a good many cuts above the sort of local bard you find slouching in some backwater tavern. A shade too barbaric for most of my colleagues; but, I've always thought that a touch of splendid barbarity livens up a tale."

Lucian's dour spirits lifted as the *lyrikos* hobbled forward. Cradling an instrument whose sidepieces curved like warriors' bows, he brushed his fingers across the strings, and silvery notes rippled through the tent. Gold-Horse raised his head. His back straightened, his eyes brightened, and his voice rang as if he were still in the strength of his young manhood.

"This is a story of Lord Yellow-Mane, mightiest warrior of all the Horse Clans," he began. "The tale of his last and greatest battle."

"These old geezers do quite well at this sort of thing," Fronto remarked to Lucian. "It should be marvelously gory, swords clashing, fellows cloven to the chine— whatever a *chine* may be."

"There are battles of many kinds," said Gold-Horse, silencing Fronto with a glance, "some calling for more courage than others. Be you the judge of this one.

"In that time, Mother Earth was but a half-grown girl," Gold-Horse continued. "There were few meadows of sweet grass, few streams of water, and the stony fields yielded barely enough to keep men and animals from hunger. Tribes fought each other to the death over a scrap of pasture and shed more blood than the water they gained from the shallowest brook.

"Now, Lord Yellow-Mane was the strongest and wisest of chieftains, vigilant to defend the lives and well-being of his clan and kindred. With his great bow that he alone could draw, his arrows that flew true to their mark, his sword that never lost its edge, and his unbreakable shield, he and his war band withstood every foe.

"Yet, on a certain day, his old enemy, Lord Quick-to-Strike, armed himself and his warriors and challenged Yellow-Mane to mortal combat. Though such rashness puzzled him, for the sake of honor Yellow-Mane could not refuse. Nevertheless, on the eve of battle, his spirit was troubled; and, sleepless, he sat before his tent, pondering deeply.

" 'Why does Quick-to-Strike seek combat?' he wondered. 'My warriors far outnumber his, our victory is assured. What drives him to such folly? Has he gained some secret power unknown to me?'

"As Yellow-Mane sat alone with his thoughts, his beloved steed, Cloud-Rising, white as snowcapped Mount Panthea, beautiful as sunlight on morning grass, trotted up, laid her head on his shoulder, and spoke softly to him.

" 'Even you, Lord, in your wisdom,' she said, 'have not seen to the heart of the matter. Quick-to-Strike does have a secret power: the strength of desperation. What drives him is not folly but starvation. He must risk all or his people will surely perish of hunger and thirst. Would you, Lord, not do likewise?'

" 'Yes,' replied Yellow-Mane, 'and his despair makes him all the more dangerous. Therefore, I must fight him fiercely lest he destroy my people. This is my obligation and first duty to my clan. Even so, my heart aches; for this will not be battle but slaughter. I see no other course.'

" 'Always have I done your bidding,' said Cloud-Rising, 'and always have you trusted me to do so. Now I ask you to do my bidding in all things, exactly as I shall tell you.'

"Yellow-Mane gave his word. But when Cloud-Rising bade him follow her, he hesitated a moment. 'The morning of battle draws near,' he said. 'I must be at the head of my war band.'

" 'So you shall,' said Cloud-Rising. 'Where we go there is neither time nor space. When the moment comes, you shall be at the forefront of the fray.' "

"Now we're getting down to it," whispered Fronto. "We'll soon have heads rolling, chines cloven—strong stuff, but don't let it upset you. It's only a story."

"Yes, and I want to listen," replied Lucian. "I've never heard one like it before. So, please, Fronto, if you don't mind—"

"Yellow-Mane then mounted his faithful steed," Gold-Horse went on, "and instantly she soared through the air as if she had grown wings. When she touched earth again, Yellow-Mane found himself in a land he had never seen before. In front of him rose a wall of fire blazing so fiercely that Yellow-Mane, brave though he was, drew back from it.

" 'Pass through it without fear,' said Cloud-Rising. 'But

what you must know is this: As fire eats all it touches, so it will consume all your joy of battle and of setting your strength against others.'

" 'I am a warrior,' said Yellow-Mane, 'and have always gone eagerly and happily to the fray. Such has been my nature. To lose that is to lose the very warp and weft of my being.'

" 'Turn back if you choose,' said Cloud-Rising, 'but what you will gain will be greater than what you lose.'

"And Yellow-Mane passed through the flames. As he felt his pride as a warrior burn away, he understood it had been only ashes to begin with.

"Next, Cloud-Rising led him to a great waterfall, a roaring cataract so high that Yellow-Mane could not glimpse the source of it. Again, he hesitated and drew back from the thundering waters.

" 'Pass through it without fear,' said Cloud-Rising, 'but what you must know is this: As a flood sweeps away all in its path, so will this torrent sweep away all striving for power and predominance.'

" 'I am a chieftain,' said Yellow-Mane. 'My striving is for my people above all. Without that, how shall I lead them?'

" 'Turn back if you choose,' said Cloud-Rising, 'but what you will gain will be greater than what you lose.'

"And Yellow-Mane passed through the rushing waters. As they swept away the power he had so striven for, he understood it had been no more than a bubble borne away on the tide."

"Where's the gore?" said Fronto under his breath. "Not a drop, so far."

"Cloud-Rising then led Yellow-Mane across a field to a high tent, where sat a man wrapped in robes and blankets. A mask of painted wood covered his face. With artistry such as Yellow-Mane had never seen, the man was carving dolls in the shapes of men and women. Yet as soon as he finished one, he would break it and cast it aside.

"When Yellow-Mane cried out at seeing marvelous handiwork so treated, the doll maker replied: 'As they are mine to make, so are they mine to break.'

"Then, with his knife, the doll maker drew a circle in the dust and within it set many tiny figures on horseback. He beckoned Yellow-Mane to look closely at them.

" 'They are warriors arrayed for battle,' said Yellow-Mane. 'I see the faces of my war band, and myself leading them. There, too, is Quick-to-Strike and his men.'

"The doll maker, in one movement of his hand, swept all these figures together in a heap. 'Now, Yellow-Mane,' he said, 'sort them out, one from the other, friend from foe.'

" 'Easily done,' said Yellow-Mane. Yet try as he may,

they all appeared alike to him. 'I cannot,' he said at last. 'How can they be sorted when among them is no difference?'

" 'Go from here,' said the doll maker. 'If you have understood what you have seen, you will know what you must do.'

"Yellow-Mane mounted his steed again and, that instant, found himself at the head of his war band. Now came Quick-to-Strike with his own men ready to battle. But Yellow-Mane galloped forward and halted between the two lines of warriors.

" 'I will raise no hand against you,' Yellow-Mane called out as Quick-to-Strike rode up, sword unsheathed, to join combat. 'To slay you is to slay myself as well. Your warriors and mine are not two tribes, but one people of one body. Does a man cut off his own limbs or plunge a blade into his own heart? Let us join together in peace.'

" 'I have no thirst for blood,' replied Quick-to-Strike. 'But it is easy for you to cry peace when your weapons are greater than mine, and with them, you may turn upon us whenever you please.'

" 'Behold, then, what I do,' said Yellow-Mane, 'in token of good faith. My warriors shall do likewise, and so shall yours.'

"With that, Yellow-Mane flung his great bow high into the air, drew his arrows from their quiver and scattered them to the wind. He plunged his sword into the ground up to its hilt, and cast aside his shield.

"Seeing this, his warriors cried out in dismay. But Quick-to-Strike nodded agreement, saying, 'I and my warriors will do the same, but on this condition: Your sacrifice must be complete. One last thing must be added: your war horse, Cloud-Rising.'

" 'No,' retorted Yellow-Mane. 'This I will not.'

" 'Yellow-Mane,' said Cloud-Rising, 'you promised to do my bidding. Now I bid you: Take my life, or all else goes for naught.'

"Yellow-Mane's heart shattered in his breast. Yet he had given his word. So he took the sword from the hands of Quick-to-Strike. Turning his face away, in a single sweep of the blade he slew Cloud-Rising.

"No sooner had a drop of her blood touched the earth than a fountain of clear water gushed from the spot. His sword rose up as a tree laden with white blossoms. Where Yellow-Mane's arrows had fallen sprang shoots of tender grass. Where his shield lay, there spread a lake sparkling like crystal; and, where he had flung his bow into the sky, now arched a rainbow.

"And, that same instant, Cloud-Rising became a

winged maiden garbed in shining white robes. Smiling with love, she took the hand of Yellow-Mane and bore him upward with her, higher and higher, until they vanished from sight.

"Some say that Cloud-Rising was Woman-Three-Women in maidenly guise; others, that she was a sun-daughter and took Yellow-Mane to dwell in a golden tent, and they ride Father Sun's horses each day from dawn to dusk; still others give different accounts. Who can tell? All truth is one truth. And so it is that the Horse Clan follows the path of peace."

Gold-Horse set aside his instrument and bowed his head, and his years once again cloaked him. Fronto was loudly snuffling and blubbering as huge teardrops poured from his eyes and streamed down his nose.

"Too much, too much!" he wailed. "I couldn't bear it when Yellow-Mane slew Cloud-Rising. I know it's only a story; but, in my present state, I don't want to hear of such things happening, as it were, to my kinfolk. Dear Lucian, be so kind as to fetch me another basin of mare's milk."

"Thank you for the tale," said Lucian as Gold-Horse approached to offer courtesies. "It was beautiful, and more than that. A gift I'll never forget."

"I am grateful," said Gold-Horse. "As for you," he

added, taking Fronto's head between his hands and looking deeply into his eyes, "yes, I do see a poet in there. I
hope for your successful transformation. I fear, however,
that you may always remain something of an ass."

15

The Game of Warriors

The feasting, with more dancing and music, kept on well past daybreak. Fronto, having investigated several basins of mare's milk, snuffled about for yet another. Lucian would have gladly crawled under a blanket to sleep; but Swift-Arrow, still fresh-eyed, jumped up, stripped off his shirt, and called for his comrades to fetch their horses.

"My young hotheads will play the Game of Warriors," See-Far-Ahead explained. "Their blood stirs, and better for them to sport than quarrel."

"Local custom?" said Fronto, belching luxuriously. "Always interested in local customs. Because, you see, they're so interesting."

"What kind of game?" asked Lucian.

"A simple one," replied Swift-Arrow, smiling. "Horsemen gather within a circle. A leather ball stuffed with grass is put in play. Each rider strives to seize and carry it past the boundary."

"That's all?"

"No rider may dismount," said Swift-Arrow. "If he leaves his horse's back for any reason, he forfeits the game. That is the one and only rule. A harmless amusement, but it demands a small measure of strength and skill. It might please you to observe our sport—from a comfortable distance."

"It might please me even more," said Lucian, returning Swift-Arrow's glance, "to try this harmless amusement. I'd enjoy it."

"Your presence would honor us," replied Swift-Arrow as Lucian began peeling off his shirt. "We shall find a gentle old nag that will suit you best."

"Here, here, no need for that," put in Fronto. "I'll be delighted to serve. I'd enjoy a little romp. This delicious beverage has made me feel marvelously light-footed."

Swift-Arrow burst out laughing. "A jackass? In the noble game?"

"You told me there was only one rule," said Lucian. "I'll ride Fronto."

"A jackass, then. Perhaps two." Swift-Arrow strode from the tent and whistled for his horse. Joy-in-the-

Dance seemed about to speak; but Lucian turned on his heel and hurried after the warrior. Licking up the last few drops from the basin, Fronto trotted eagerly to join them.

The dance ground had been cleared, and a circle had been marked out. The folk of the camp made way for the riders. Lucian, perched on Fronto, entered the ring, and the onlookers closed ranks. A young boy ran up with a ball several times larger than Lucian's head and, at a signal from Swift-Arrow, tossed it into the ring.

The warriors all seemed to go mad at that same instant, whooping and yip-yipping, yelling and screaming until Lucian feared his ears would split. Fronto burst into raucous hee-haws and went lurching toward the wheeling, rearing horses. One rider had already leaned from his mount and snatched up the ball, which was attached to long, rawhide loops. As he made for the boundary, the whole band galloped straight for him, jostling their steeds against his, jabbing him with elbows and fists, and, by sheer force, knocking the ball from his grasp. When a second rider scooped it up, he, too, was kicked and pummeled until he dropped it.

"All against all, every man for himself?" Lucian felt his blood rising. "Well, then: Yip-yip-yip!"

Fronto needed no urging. His eyes lit up, he laid back

his ears and, braying wildly, plunged into the fray. Shorter and closer to the ground than the horses, the poet darted in and out among them, dodging and wheeling with joyous abandon.

Deafened by the endless whooping and pounding hooves, Lucian's head spun as he found himself buffeted from all sides. The flank of one horse crashed broadside against him; an elbow jabbed him in the face, he choked and snorted at the blood streaming from his nose. A couple of riders had been knocked off their mounts and, in penalty, were sent from the ring. Though infuriated at being so belabored, Lucian was afraid of losing his own seat. Seeking a moment to get back his breath and his balance, he pulled away from the press of warriors. The ball, at the same time, rolled clear of the struggling riders.

"I have it!" cried Lucian, about to seize the rawhide loop.

"First, a little poetic license," said Fronto as the warriors, losing sight of the ball, milled around in all directions. Straddling the object as if he were hatching an oversized egg, Fronto trapped it between his hind legs and waddled toward the edge of the ring.

"They can't find it. Pick it up now," ordered Fronto. "We'll make a run for it."

Lucian snatched the ball from under Fronto's belly. The other players, by this time, had seen him do so. All bore down on him in full whoop, Swift-Arrow grinning in the lead.

Bracing himself for the assault, Lucian clapped his heels against Fronto's flanks. The poet stood motionless.

"Go! Go!" shouted Lucian.

Fronto did not budge, his eyes set on Swift-Arrow's mount. "Why, that's one of the mares that took such a fancy to me. And there's another. Good morning, ladies."

Swift-Arrow's steed gave a flirtatious whinny as she plunged toward Fronto. When she reached him, she stopped so abruptly that Swift-Arrow sailed head over heels to land heavily on the turf; likewise, the riders behind him.

"Later, perhaps, my dear," said Fronto as she fondly nuzzled him. He made for the boundary at a wobbling gallop, with Lucian still clutching the ball. The spectators laughed and cheered. Swift-Arrow, climbing to his feet, looked as if he had swallowed a porcupine.

"Well done, my boy," said Fronto. "What an exhilarating sport! Brightens the eye, sets the pulse racing and the blood coursing."

"It certainly does," Lucian agreed, "and I don't ever want to play it again."

"I hope those mares won't come looking for me," said Fronto.

That night, at a special feast to celebrate the occasion,

See-Far-Ahead declared Lucian and Fronto honorary members of the Horse Clan.

"Never have I seen our game won in so unusual a fashion," the chieftain said. "I congratulate you. And I thank you. It is good for my hotheads to have their pride cooled a little."

See-Far-Ahead called for pots of color and daubed clan markings on Lucian's forehead and cheeks, and on the nose and brow of Fronto.

"Does this make me an honorary horse?" said the poet. "That's a step up from jackass."

"Aiee-Ouch," said Joy-in-the-Dance, drawing Lucian aside, "I have a couple of things I want to tell you."

"Oh?" Lucian, beaming with happy satisfaction, had decided to accept her humble apology, generously forgive her, and bask in her adoration at his triumph.

"Aiee-Ouch, what you did," Joy-in-the-Dance began, "I can only say—well, it was the most foolhardy, dangerous, silliest, stupidest—"

"Was it?" Lucian abruptly stopped basking. Instead, he bristled. "I'd call it a matter of honor. Besides," he added under his breath, "I won."

"Aside from pointing out that you could have broken your neck," she went on, "what I mainly wanted to say —I hope you managed to see why I didn't tell you who I was."

"I don't know—All right, I suppose I did."

Joy-in-the-Dance took his hand. "I thought you would."

"So the two of you are on fond terms again," Fronto remarked later. "That's gratifying."

"Yes," said Lucian, "but I really hate it when she's right."

※

See-Far-Ahead decided that he would go with his daughter to Mount Panthea. Leaving the camp in charge of Swift-Arrow, he picked half a dozen of his warriors to journey with him, ordered his tent struck and provisions loaded onto pack animals. Joy-in-the-Dance, lightly astride a slender white mare, rode beside her father's black stallion. Swift-Arrow, having made a sour sort of peace with Lucian, offered him a sturdy chestnut-and-white pony and provided Ops with a similar mount.

Lucian was not sure how thankful he should be to Swift-Arrow. For the first few days, he was too sore to sit down and no less so when he stood up. He never acquired a taste for being bounced and battered and having his teeth rattled at every jolt. Even when he could gallop over the grasslands, yip-yipping as well as any of the warriors, he would not have chosen to be a permanent member of the Horse Clan.

"You're a long way from bean counting," said Fronto, observing the daubs of color still vivid on Lucian's face, and his skin broiled nearly black from the unclouded sun. "My boy, you're turning into quite the picturesque barbarian—and, as a poet, I've found that a touch of wildness never goes amiss, especially with the ladies."

"Picturesque barbarian?" Lucian shook his head. "I don't know what I am. Or what I'll be." He turned to Ops, who was looking thoughtfully at the snowcapped peak of Mount Panthea rising just ahead. "And you, Ops? What will you ask the Lady? Is there something she could grant you?"

"I doubt it," said the scapegoat. "Oh, perhaps more opportunity to be of service. Not so much wandering at random. It's hit or miss, finding people to blame something on you. Yes, I would like a steadier occupation."

"That's a modest request," said Joy-in-the-Dance, joining them in time to hear this remark by Ops. "I hope my mother will be able to grant it."

The girl, throughout these days, had stayed a little apart, withdrawn into her own thoughts. Now Lucian ventured to go and sit beside her.

"You'll soon see your mother. You'll be glad of that, won't you?"

"Yes. But I still wonder if I did right, not changing the prophecy. She's the only one who can tell me. If I did wrong, I'll have a lot to answer for." She smiled at him. "I can't guess what she'll say to my bringing along an Aiee-Ouch."

"Does it matter?"

"No. Not anymore. Did you think it would?"

"I hoped not," said Lucian.

Next day, they came to the sanctuary of the Lady of Wild Things.

16

The Lady of Wild Things

All that morning, See-Far-Ahead had borne westward over gently rising foothills, and across the shallowest ford of a wide river. Soon the ground fell sharply away, and at the foot of Mount Panthea, Lucian glimpsed clustered buildings of white stone, colonnades and walkways, groves and gardens in full blossom. What held his eyes and astonished him all the more was an enclosure of tall columns, some broken and lying on the expanse of rutted stone steps. Of what had been a roof, only the high-peaked forefront remained. Even from these ruins, he could imagine what the building once had been; the grace of its design and proportions made him catch his breath in wonder. Massive though they were, the columns seemed light enough to soar into the air and float away.

"This must be the work of the Great Ones," he murmured. "Who else? They truly lived here once, just as Joy-in-the-Dance told us."

"No doubt," said Fronto. "No one today could build anything like it. In comparison, the palace of Bromios comes off like an oversized rabbit warren."

As the travelers entered a grove of poplars, a number of young women in white tunics greeted them, happily embracing Joy-in-the-Dance and leading her and the warriors down a wide avenue. When Lucian, Fronto, and Ops attempted to follow, one of the maidens stepped in front of them.

"The Lady will send word when she wishes to see you," said the girl, who gave her name as Laurel-Crown. Auburn-haired, with a narrow band of gold at her brow, she nodded courteously to Lucian and Fronto; her full gaze lingered, however, on Ops, and she looked him up and down with unconcealed interest. For his part, Ops did something Lucian had never seen him do: He blushed crimson to the roots of his hair and the tips of his ears.

"I'm to stay with you until you're called for," said Laurel-Crown, her hazel eyes still on the scapegoat. "It

may be a little while. I can show you some of the sanctuary, if you'd like. It's quite lovely."

"What I've seen is most attractive," replied Ops, giving the maiden a few sidelong glances of his own.

"You're speaking of the ruins?" said Laurel-Crown.
"There are other things, as well."

"Indeed there are," said Ops. "I hope to grow better
acquainted with them."

"That," Laurel-Crown said primly, "would depend on
what you have in mind."

"I don't think they're talking about ruins and sight-
seeing," Lucian said under his breath to Fronto.

"That rascal Ops," Fronto chuckled as Laurel-Crown
led the way to a fountain and pool. "Who'd have thought
it of him? He no sooner sets foot here than a young lady
takes a shine to him, and he to her. At first sight!"

"It happened to his parents," Lucian said. "Maybe it
runs in the family."

While Ops watered the horses, Lucian noticed
women of every age strolling along walkways or talking
together on marble benches. "Do they all serve the Lady?"
he asked Laurel-Crown.

"No," she said, momentarily turning her glance away
from Ops, "they've come to take refuge since Bromios
began persecuting them. Only the Daughters of Morning,

like me, and the Moon Maidens serve the Lady as her chosen companions."

"But men and boys are forbidden here?"

"Of course not, if they're followers of the Lady. We have infants, too, though only a few right now. All women are free to bring their children to be raised among us. Their sons often become village chiefs when they're grown. Their daughters, if they choose, study our mysteries, then return home to teach them to other women; or, if they show promise, stay to become Moon Maidens or Daughters of Morning. At least, that's how it was until Bromios took power. Now it may be that our sisterhood is broken. Of that, even the Lady isn't certain."

Other Daughters of Morning, carrying baskets of food and drink, had come, trailed by a crowd of younger girls eager to see a talking donkey. Giggling and nudging one another, they pressed around Fronto, patting his head and urging him to speak. Some had woven wildflower garlands to hang around his neck or drape over his ears.

Lucian and Ops, likewise, were objects of curiosity. Taken at first for one of the Horse Clan, Lucian explained that he was only an honorary member, then wished he had said nothing, for the girls drew back, round-eyed and fearful.

"They have never seen a man of the Bear people,"

said Laurel-Crown, "but they know what happened here long ago."

"Which is more than I do," said Lucian.

"Haven't you been told your own history?"

"Not that part of it," said Lucian, "but I'd like to find out. Would you tell me?"

Laurel-Crown hesitated. "It's a story that won't please you."

"Even so," Lucian insisted, "I still want to hear it."

"As you wish," said Laurel-Crown.

"Generations ago," she continued, "when your first Bear King conquered Arkadia Beyond-the-Mountains, he journeyed here to seek audience with the Lady of Wild Things.

"With gentle speech and honeyed words, he paid homage to her beauty and wisdom and claimed that he desired to learn her peaceable ways.

" 'Your purpose is commendable,' said the Lady. 'Only tell me this: Why have you brought your war band with you?'

" 'Lady, these are my close companions. I wish them, as well as I, to benefit from your teachings.'

" 'So be it,' said the Lady. 'I will not deny knowledge to any who truly seek it. Only tell me this: Why come you armed with sword and spear, and your companions likewise?'

" 'Lady, to defend ourselves against peril on our way.'

" 'So be it,' said the Lady. 'Then let us begin your instruction. As you have studied the arts of war, now shall you study the arts of peace.'

"With that, she led him to her spinning chamber, bade him to take up wool and distaff, teasel and spindle, and to sit at her wheel and spin thread.

" 'You ask this of me?' cried the Bear King. 'Lady, I am a warrior and do not turn my hand to women's work. If my men were to see me like some handmaiden at a spinning wheel, they would laugh me to scorn.'

"The Lady did not insist but next led him to her stables, bidding him to sweep them clean, to feed and groom her horses.

" 'You ask this of me?' he cried. 'Lady, I am a king and this is labor for baseborn servants. Set me a task worthy of my rank, my strength of arm, and my fleetness of foot.'

" 'So be it,' said the Lady. 'Will you run a race against me? If you win, all my wisdom and secret knowledge will be granted to you.'

" 'That is a suitable challenge,' said the Bear King, for he knew that none was swifter than himself. 'I gladly accept.'

"So saying, he stripped off helmet and breastplate and laid down spear and sword. The Lady, having girt up her tunic, marked out the course, the Daughters of Morning lining one side, the king's war band on the other. And so began the race.

"Quick as wind ran the Lady of Wild Things and, at first, outpaced the Bear King. But he, bending all his strength, drew ever closer, closing the distance between them, gaining on her stride by stride.

"Now, the Lady of Wild Things had seen into the Bear King's heart and well knew that his purpose was not the gaining of wisdom but the conquest of her domain. Therefore, from the folds of her garment she drew an apple fashioned of purest gold and dropped it on the ground behind her.

"At sight of the precious object glittering in his path, the Bear King broke stride and eagerly snatched it up. In that instant of his delay, the Lady of Wild Things pressed ahead, speeding first to the finish of the course. The Bear King shook his fist and roared in fury.

" 'Woman's treachery and deception! Victory should have been mine. You have cheated me.'

" 'You have cheated yourself,' replied the Lady. 'Your own greed blinded you, and you chose to seize what lay nearest at hand, heedless of the farther goal. You dare cry treachery and deception? No, it was you who came with a man's fair speech and false heart.'

" 'Here, let this be your prize,' cried the Bear King,

and he picked up his spear and flung it straight at her breast. But it struck the amulet she wore around her neck, the spearhead shattered, and the shaft fell to the ground.

"In rage, the Bear King and his warriors drew their swords and would have slain the Lady and her maidens had they not sought refuge amid the crags of Mount Panthea. Unable to attack them in their mountain fastness, the king and his war band pillaged the great sanctuary, seizing all volumes of lore and learning, intending to possess these secrets. But the mysteries had been written in Mother Tongue, which the Bear men could not read. And so they spitefully burned every book, every scroll, then toppled the columns, shattered the roof, and wrought all destruction they could.

"The Lady sent an eagle bearing word to her beloved friend, Lord Yellow-Mane, who led his Horse Clan against the Bear King and his men and put them to flight.

"Although the books had been burned past recovery, the Lady and her maidens remembered all their contents. However, the Lady vowed that none of the lore should be written down again but kept only in memory and handed down by word of mouth. Thus, it could never be stolen or destroyed, or turned to evil ends."

"Joy-in-the-Dance told us that your knowledge was no longer put in writing," said Lucian. "So that's how it came about." He had listened to the tale with fascination; at the same time, it had made his heart heavy with grief and shame for what the Bear men had done. "I see why you don't write down your mysteries, but why was the sanctuary never rebuilt?"

"It cannot be," said Laurel-Crown. "Its marble came from one place only: the cliffs near Metara. That's the finest in Arkadia, no other is worthy to be used. But we don't venture into the realm of our enemies. So the ruins remain as you see them, a symbol of Bear men's perfidy."

"I very dimly recall my mother telling me that story," said Ops to Laurel-Crown. "In Mother Tongue, at the time—Ah, it's been so long since I've heard or spoken the language that I've forgotten it—but I well remember my mother's voice. She was a sanctuary maiden, you see, and what happened—"

"Please, Ops," said Fronto, "don't go into all that tootling and bleating again."

"I'd love to hear more," said Laurel-Crown, glancing at Ops with even warmer interest. "Let's sit over there while your friends do something to occupy themselves and leave us—"

Laurel-Crown broke off, for one of the Daughters of Morning had come to say that the Lady of Wild Things waited to receive them. With the moment upon him, Lucian's uneasiness sprang up to entangle itself with his hopes as he followed the maiden through a colonnade and into a sunny courtyard. In the center of it a fountain played; nearby, on a marble bench sat a woman draped in a pale blue robe. At her feet stretched two sleek leopards lazily observing the new arrivals.

Joy-in-the-Dance, garbed in a fresh white tunic, sat beside her mother. See-Far-Ahead, arms folded, stood behind them. The Lady of Wild Things beckoned with an easy gesture. She wore no rings on her slender fingers, nor bracelets on her bare arms. Her only jewels were the brooch of amethyst at her shoulder knot and the silver diadem, set with a single gem, holding her long, golden hair. Joy-in-the-Dance gave Lucian a quick smile, and he thought, "She has her mother's eyes."

The Lady's glance lingered a moment on Lucian, then she looked past him at Ops, who had hung back a little.

"*Khaire*, Argeus Bright-Face," she said in a kindly voice. "You are under my protection and welcome here. By mother-right, you may count this place your home."

She now set a stern gaze on Fronto, whose four legs began to quake. "I know what has befallen you, by your own doing. Come to me, poet. Only at my daughter's entreaty have I agreed to see you."

"Honored Lady, my deepest gratitude, heartfelt thanks," Fronto stammered, bending his trembling forelegs in an attempt to kneel, "and may I say that for one so youthful to have a grown daughter as charmingly beautiful as yourself, dear Lady, you are most amazingly—ah, unexpectedly—"

"Well preserved?" said the Lady of Wild Things. "Fronto, of all the creatures you might have become, an ass befits you most."

Fronto bowed his head. "I have been punished as I deserved. But I meant no disrespect. I sought only inspiration."

"As a poet, you should have known better than anyone," replied the Lady, "that inspiration is not found in a gulp of water or anything else. Not even I can bestow it. If it sustains you and gives you courage to imagine that I can, well and good. It is a harmless, perhaps useful, fantasy. But at the end, your inspiration must come from yourself. I can do no more than wish you well."

"I'll let my inspiration do as it pleases," said Fronto. "At the moment, I only beg your mercy and forgiveness."

"You are a poet," said the Lady, "and much foolishness is to be expected. Your intentions were good, you have always honored me, and I look kindly on your devotion. Yes, I forgive you, as I always forgive those I cherish, however asinine they may be."

"Gracious benefactress!" cried Fronto. "Thank you.

My hopes are fulfilled. Will you change me here and now? Or is some formality to be observed? A small ritual, perhaps? In any case, the sooner the better."

"What happened to you was not my doing," the Lady said, "and is not mine to undo. I cannot transform you to what you were. The first service I can offer is plain truth.

"Your time is short. You have the power of speech, but soon it must leave you. Then will you become less and less a poet and more and more a donkey, until, at last, you will be truly a dumb beast, and so remain as long as you draw breath."

17

The Shipmaster

The Lady of Wild Things fell silent. In the sun-washed courtyard, the only sound was the splashing water of the fountain. The leopards licked their paws. Fronto lowered his head and turned away.

"All for naught," he murmured. "My last hope gone."

"There is always hope, however slight," the Lady said. "I have told you the worst, so that you may truly know the gravity of your situation.

"I have thought carefully on this," she went on. "Ancient lore tells of other means of restoration, seldom used, if ever; for, most often, they destroy instead of cure. You would not like them, Fronto, and I counsel you against them."

"I'll take any risk," said Fronto. "I could hardly be worse off."

"Yes, you could," said the Lady. "Would you accept, for example, to be set on a blazing pyre, with no assurance of surviving that ordeal? Or, if you did, with the likelihood of emerging in a shape more unbearable than your present one? I assure you, compared with other methods, that is the least painful. Or would you choose to have all the blood drained from your body, and then—"

"Please, please, say no more," wailed Fronto. "I catch your drift."

"One possibility remains," the Lady continued. "It is the most promising. An island named Callista lies off the southern coast, unspoiled by the coming of the Bear folk. Some of the Great Ones' magic still flourishes there. A water-maiden guards a pool much like the one at Mount Lerna. Journey to Callista. In my name, ask her help. She will, on my authority, permit you to bathe in the waters. The chances are excellent that they will transform you."

"Bless you, dear Lady!" cried Fronto, his spirits lifting. "That is, thank you for blessing me with your kindness."

"Be warned," said the Lady of Wild Things. "I told you that your time is short. By my reckoning, you have until the first full moon of the Harvest Festival. However, you should reach Callista before that if you sail without delay."

"How can we find it?" put in Lucian. "How can we even get there? Without a boat—"

"I shall take up that matter once I have dealt with you, Lucian, who my daughter, for reasons of her own, prefers to call Aiee-Ouch.

"I permitted you to come here because of your care and affection for this wretched poet. Now you must leave and never set foot here again. I offer no welcome to my enemies."

"I'm not your enemy," Lucian replied heatedly, despite his attempt to hold back his anger and resentment. "Do you judge every Bear man alike? That's not much different from Bromios, only the other way round." He stopped short and bit his lips, fearing he had dared to go too far.

"He speaks truth," See-Far-Ahead said quietly. "My heart aches when I think of the long hatred between you and the Bear tribe."

"With good cause," said the Lady of Wild Things. "Once, there might have been friendship. That is no longer possible."

"I know it's possible," said Joy-in-the-Dance, to Lucian's astonishment. "Aiee-Ouch and I—" She halted as color rose to her cheeks. "I mean, it's a beginning—"

"Which must end when he departs," said the Lady. She turned again to Lucian. "My daughter has told me that you seek to know what shape your life should take. It is beyond even my knowledge to answer such a question. You alone must learn that for yourself."

"Then we've come here in vain," Lucian said bitterly. "If you have no help for me, so be it. As for Fronto, all you've done is tell him about an island we don't know how to find, and can't reach in the first place. You give him hope and take it away. That's cruel—"

"You speak with more haste than judgment," said the Lady. "For the sake of this poet, I will grant a favor larger than you might expect from one you call cruel. In the harbor, at the foot of the cliffs, there is a fishing village. Its folk have dwelt in our care from long before the days of the Bear kings. Among them lives a shipmaster, Oudeis. A seafarer of great skill, he knows the waters from here to Callista and can set the swiftest course."

The Lady took an amulet and chain from the folds of her robe and set it around Lucian's neck. "Show him this. He will do all you ask."

"I'll gladly go along," said Ops before Lucian could reply. "If the wind dies or the boat leaks, they'll need someone to blame. A wonderful opportunity for me."

"No, Argeus Bright-Face," the Lady said. "Your place is here. My daughter has told me of your request. I must give it long and careful thought. Be patient and stay among us until I see what is best for you."

"I've brought Aiee-Ouch and Fronto this far," declared Joy-in-the-Dance. "I'll certainly go the rest of the way with them."

"No, you shall not," replied the Lady, as Lucian's heart sank. "It is not fitting. Now leave us, child," the Lady went on. "Take Argeus Bright-Face to his chambers, then remain in your own."

The girl's chin shot up. Her eyes and the Lady's met and locked. "I do not speak as a mother to a beloved daughter," the Lady said in a low voice, "but as the Lady of Wild Things to her pythoness. Do as I say. You know that you must."

Joy-in-the-Dance stood, as if she would step toward Lucian, then turned abruptly, head high, and strode from the courtyard. Ops followed. Lucian started after her. The Lady rose to stand in front of him. The leopards, alert, twitched their tails.

Lucian faced the Lady of Wild Things. "Let me say farewell to her. That much, at least."

"No," the Lady said. "Do you think me heartless? I am not. I am doing you a kindness. It would be too painful for both of you.

"I will tell you this," she added. "My daughter was torn in spirit when she came here and questioned whether she should have changed the prophecy she gave your king. I have made it clear to her. By speaking the true prophecy she proved herself worthy of her rank. She is a pythoness. That is her life. You can have no part in it."

❦

He was filled with her absence and might as well have been sleepwalking for all the heed he paid to where he was being led. Laurel-Crown had been instructed to guide him and Fronto down the cliffs to the fishing village, where she pointed out the shipmaster's hut, and left them there.

"Hurry along, my boy," urged the poet. "Glooming never mended a broken heart, as I've discovered a thousand times. Think of something else. Anything. Go alphabetically. Anthills. Beetles. Callista—Ah, that's a happy prospect.

"We'll go in style, too." Fronto tossed his head toward a little cove and a sleek, high-masted ship. "This what's his name—Oudeis—let's get him stirring, reef the anchor, hoist the rudder, whatever these nautical fellows do."

Fronto eagerly trotted across the threshold of the hut. Lucian, at his heels, was surprised to find that the hut was more spacious on the inside than it appeared from the outside. The reason, he understood, was that the chamber had been so cleverly laid out. Tables and benches of polished wood had been set into the walls; what looked like a fishnet was slung between two beams of a ceiling crafted of wooden ribs. Storage bins nested one on top of the other; an oil lamp hung from a chain. Only one thing seemed to be missing: the occupant.

"I hope he's not gone far," said Fronto. "We've no time to lose. Seek him out, lad, at the piers; perhaps the local tavern, or whatever sort of place might attract the seafaring trade."

The words had barely passed his lips when a voice boomed from the doorway: "A jackass! Away with you, lumbering lummox!"

A figure as high and wide as the doorway itself dropped the wineskin he carried on his shoulder. With hardly a glance at Lucian, he seized Fronto by the ears and would have hauled him bodily from the hut if Lucian had not brandished the amulet. At sight of it, the man stopped and drew back a pace.

"What are you up to with that?"

"Are you the shipmaster?" Lucian stepped between him and Fronto. "Oudeis?"

"Who else?" The man loomed bulkier than Bromios, with a salt-and-pepper beard in tight curls, hair closely cropped, a jutting hawk's beak of a nose, and shrewd black eyes flecked with gold. "And you? Is that your jack-ass? Yes, well, take that sorry bone bag away before he makes a mess on my floor."

"My good shipmaster," said Fronto, tossing his head and looking down his nose, "credit me with at least a measure of refinement. I'm not what I appear to be. Has it not occurred to you that I can speak?"

"I don't care a fig if you can whistle out your ears," retorted Oudeis. "Make a mess, you clean it up. What do you want? The quicker you tell me, the quicker you're gone."

Fearing the testy Oudeis would throw him out the door despite the amulet, Lucian hurried to explain their circumstances. The shipmaster's weather-beaten face fell, he scratched his beard, puffed his cheeks, and muttered to himself.

"The Lady told us you'd do as we ask," Lucian insisted.

"I will," grumbled Oudeis. "I owe her more service than I can repay. There's been times when she's held my life in the palm of her hand. Aye, her spirit bore me up, else I'd have drowned a dozen times over. I'll take you where you want to go. That doesn't mean I have to like it. I've shipped many a strange cargo in my day, but never a jackass, let alone a talking one."

"I assure you," said Fronto, "on our return voyage,

when I'm back to myself, you'll find me most entertaining. Once my difficulty is resolved and my mind can concentrate on my profession, I'll compose a few rhymes to amuse a seafaring fellow like yourself—though unsuitable for the ears of your lady wife. On that subject, we have not had the pleasure of her acquaintance."

"For good reason," Oudeis replied. "There isn't one. I lost my best chance these long years past." He sighed, his eyes wandered an instant. Then, with a shrug, he went to fetch a smooth, flat board.

"I regret to hear that," said Fronto, "and I'm astonished, as well. Your snug abode betokens a feminine hand."

"Only mine. I keep my little haven shipshape. I'm the one who built what you see here. Aye, and devised it all myself." This while, the shipmaster had been unfolding wooden poles neatly joined and hinged into the board; within the moment, there stood a table.

"Remarkable!" exclaimed Lucian, intrigued and delighted.

The shipmaster beamed proudly. "I wasn't called Clever Oudeis for nothing. You won't find a better mariner, if I say so myself. Besides that, there's not a task, a piece of work, I can't do.

"Now, then, as for Callista," he went on, drawing up stools for Lucian and himself while Fronto thrust his head over Lucian's shoulder, "let's do a little reckoning. I'll have to lay in provisions, water, extra gear. Some few chores to finish. Aye, all told, we'll set sail in, say, five or six days."

"What?" burst out Fronto. "We can't possibly wait that long."

"You're not only a jackass, you're a landlubber as well," Oudeis retorted. "Go off ill-fitted? Do you suppose I'll risk my neck and my ship? Not counting your necks—which, I'll tell you frankly, don't weigh heavy in comparison. No. Out of the question."

"I wouldn't dream of doubting your judgment." Lucian put up his hands in resignation. "You know your trade. A week? A month, if need be," he added as Fronto stared aghast. "We'll have to wait, since that's the best you can manage. I understand now. Calling yourself Clever Oudeis was only a fanciful manner of speaking."

"Fact!" Oudeis slapped a heavy hand on the table. "I tell you there's nothing—" He stopped and cocked an ear, then laid a finger on his lips. He stood and pulled the netting from the beams.

"You're going fishing?" protested Fronto. "We require your undivided attention."

"Be quiet, jackass." The shipmaster went swiftly from the hut. Lucian soon heard scuffling and a few colorful oaths from Oudeis, who was back within moments, the net and its wriggling contents slung over his shoulder.

"Here's a fish for you!" Oudeis tossed his burden to the floor. "I've not seen the like of it. What is it? A creeping, crawling, eavesdropping land-fish?"

The shipmaster untangled the net.

Out popped Catch-a-Tick.

18

The Voyages of Oudeis

What are you doing here?" Lucian burst out.

"You know this wretch?" Oudeis glowered at the boy, who was swaggering around as tickled with himself as he could be. "First, a jackass. Now, a goat. Look at him, he's got mud on my floor." The shipmaster made to seize Catch-a-Tick, who stuck out his tongue and ducked behind Lucian.

"I'll deal with this," said Lucian. "How did you find us? More to the point, why did you run off? That's what you did, isn't it? Your mother must be out of her wits. Your father, too. You'll be in for a good tanning from both of them."

"No, I won't," Catch-a-Tick declared. "My mother said I could go with you."

"To Mount Panthea? I doubt that."

"All right," admitted Catch-a-Tick, "I suppose she thought I'd come straight home with the others. By the time I caught up, you'd already gone through the mountains. So, I followed. I wasn't told not to, was I? They'll guess I went with you and the pythoness. Where is she?"

"She's—staying behind. At the sanctuary."

"Well, even so," said Catch-a-Tick, "you'll take care of everything. Yes, I heard about what you did with the Horse Clan. You'd left by the time I got there, but they all talked about you. How you defeated their best warriors and—"

"And now you're going home," Lucian interrupted. "We're getting ready to sail on a journey."

"So much the better. I've never been on a ship."

"You won't be on mine," said Oudeis. "Go back wherever you came from."

Catch-a-Tick folded his arms. "If you try to leave me here, I'll swim after you."

"Please, please," said Fronto. "We'll decide what to do about him later. We have plenty of time to think it over, as we're stuck here for a week."

"Who says?" Oudeis squinted a dark eye at Lucian. "I told you I could do anything that needed doing—if I've a mind to. Well, my lad, I'll prove it to you. We sail with the night tide. I'll make do with what I have and take on the rest at one port or other. So, stir your stumps and lend a hand. The jackass, too. What about the goat-boy?"

Catch-a-Tick began whining, begging, demanding, and carrying on so much that Lucian put his hands over his ears.

"Enough! You'll come with us. Only because I want you where I can keep an eye on you. If I leave you running loose on your own, you'll get in worse trouble."

Oudeis, meantime, set about gathering what food and gear his hut offered, as well as a coarse shirt and cloak for Lucian, a blanket for Catch-a-Tick, and several wide-brimmed straw hats. Loading the cargo required a few trips between the hut and the pier, where a single-masted boat bobbed in the water. It was well after moonrise when Oudeis declared that all was to his satisfaction and ordered his passengers into the vessel.

"Cramped quarters," remarked Fronto, who had clambered unsteadily over the side. "No matter, we'll be more comfortable once we're aboard."

"Ass," retorted Oudeis, "you're aboard right now."

"But—the great ship?" cried Fronto. "We saw it in the cove."

"That's the Lady's," Oudeis said. "Not for the likes of you or me. This little beauty's mine, built with my own pair of hands."

"You didn't leave much room for your crew," said Lucian.

"What crew?" said Oudeis, casting off the mooring lines. "I'm the crew. I work my ship myself. That's not to say you lubbers will sit at ease. Put your back into those oars," he ordered Lucian and Catch-a-Tick. "Do you know what an oar is? You'll find out quick enough. Once clear of the harbor, I'll hoist sail and hope for a breeze."

Under the shipmaster's instruction, Lucian and Catch-a-Tick plied the long wooden sweeps: a labor heavier than Lucian expected. The little ship skipped along on the tide, bobbing and tossing over the gleaming black water. By the time Oudeis called a halt, Lucian's muscles were twitching in protest, and he was glad enough to rest on his oars. Oudeis, with remarkable strength, hauled on a cat's cradle of lines; and, little by little, the sail rose and spread.

"Here's for you, old Earth-Shaker," Oudeis called over the side. He unstoppered his wineskin and spilled some of its contents into the lapping waves. "Oh, I'm devoted to the Lady. But Earth-Shaker's been there long before her, long before the Great Ones. Aye, since the day the world began.

"It's a good thing to stay on the lee side of him; he's not one to trifle with. I've heard the old boy roar like thunder and send up seas high as mountains. I've seen waterspouts taller and thicker than oak trees, and whirl-pools that could suck in half a dozen ships and spit them out again."

"Even so," said Lucian, "you still follow the sea."

"And keep promising myself I'll give it up, for all the good it's brought me. Once, my home port was Metara," said Oudeis, an undertow of yearning in his voice. "Those days, I had a fine ship, with a fair business in the cargo trade. And a sweetheart. A plump, lively lass: Mir-ina was her name. We were betrothed, but I was ever putting off our wedding day. You see, I wanted to wait until my fortunes were better; for I had the notion of buying a little tavern, and the two of us running it hap-pily and handing it down to our young ones when they came along.

"One day, at the docks, a long-jawed, narrow-nosed fellow steps up to me. 'My name is Diomedes,' he says, 'and I'm told there's no better shipmaster in Metara.'

" 'Or anywhere else,' I say. 'You're not from these parts or you'd have known without being told.'

"He gives a dry sort of chuckle and nods his head. 'I'm glad I found you,' says he, 'because I want to make you a rich man.'

" 'I share your ambition for me,' say I. 'Would you care to mention how you'll do that?'

" 'Sheepskin,' says he. 'Hear me out,' he goes on, as I had started laughing in his face, sheepskins being no profitable cargo. 'I'm not talking wool, but gold. Sheepskin of pure gold.'

"That hooked my attention. All the more as he goes on to tell of a land some ways overseas, northeast of Metara; and a mighty river that washes gold down from the mountains. There, the folk lay sheepskins in the riverbed to trap the nuggets, hang the fleece to dry on trees, then comb out a treasure with no more effort than combing your hair. 'I know how to find the place,' he says, pulling out a chart. 'I and my friends propose to go and lay hands on all that fleece. You provide the ship and stores, and you'll come in for your share of the wealth. It's a speculative venture, we win all or lose all together. But,' says he, with a wink, 'I don't expect we'll lose.'

" 'It sounds like speculative robbery to me,' I answer, but he only shrugs and tells me these folk have no end of sheepskins, the river's rich, they'll never miss what's taken.

"Now, I'm no more honest than the next fellow, but I don't much care for bald-faced thievery. And yet, I was starting to think how this might be my best chance for that little tavern, to set up Mirina and me snug for the rest of our days. As those river folk have an endless golden stream, it's no great harm to them and a great good for us.

"And so—to my shame, as I'm first to admit—I agreed, and we clapped hands on the bargain. When I proposed assembling my crew, Diomedes tells me he has his own. 'And a remarkable band they are,' says he. 'Each man's as good a seafarer as you'll find, but most have yet another skill. There's a fellow with eyes keen as a lynx's—he's our lookout. There's another, quick and hard with his fists. For the heavy work, there's one so strong you'd swear he could uproot a tree as easy as you'd pull up a scallion. Have no fear, you'll never see a crew like that again.'

"I studied his chart, calculated the voyage there and back to last most likely three months, which chimed with his own reckoning. So, Diomedes goes off to gather his companions; and I take my leave of Mirina, giving her a few good swacking kisses, vowing I'll be home even before she misses me, with a fortune in my hands and a merry life for us both.

"And so we set sail, and a fair voyage it was. But, little more than halfway on our course, Diomedes sidles up to me, gives me a warm smile and a cold eye, and says, 'You've done so well for us, from here on I think we can forgo your services. What we wanted was your ship. Now we have it, no need for you.'

"I barely had time to curse myself for a gullible fool when Diomedes' bully boy—a thick-headed oaf who carried a cudgel and wore a lion's skin around his shoulders—picks me up like a feather and pitches me over the side. And the ship sails on, leaving me to the mercy of the waves.

"Much later, I heard that most of that motley crew of villains came to bad and bloody ends. Diomedes, I gather, got his sheepskin; but he took up with the daughter of one of the local worthies and there were some nasty doings in consequence. As for that lion-skinned ruffian, that's a tale in itself."

"Who cares about them?" cried Fronto. "Don't keep us hanging while you're floundering in the sea."

"I think he's doing it on purpose," whispered Lucian. "Isn't that what you called 'suspense'?"

"A little goes a long way," said Fronto. "Come on, Oudeis, you didn't drown, since you're here to tell the tale. What happened next?"

"I fought the waves and swam until I was out of strength," Oudeis continued. "Sure my end had come, I turned my last thoughts to Mirina, a widow before she was even a wife, and resigned myself to a watery grave.

"That moment, up swims the biggest dolphin I've ever seen. The Lady sent it out of mercy for me, no question about that. I flung my arms around it and climbed astride, and that blessed creature carried me on its back all day and night until we reached shore. And there it gave me a big smile and left me safe and sound.

"All along that beach, what do I see but tents and piles of gear and cook fires. And men armed to the teeth, a hundred or more, a rough-looking lot, indeed. I step up to the one who seems to be in charge, a beefy, red-faced fellow in helmet and breastplate—Strong-of-Will, as he named himself—tell him my tale, ask where I am and how I can reach Metara.

" 'You're far off your course,' says he, 'and I can't help you. I've more on my mind than a washed-up sailor.'

"He goes on to tell me they're from a kingdom a few days' voyage from here, where the king was about to marry a young maiden. 'But a youth came passing through, he and the wench took a fancy to each other. Next thing you know, they ran off and he brought her here, to his own country. My warriors and I have orders to fetch her back,' he told me.

"He points up the beach to a pretty little town overlooking the sea. 'They're behind those walls. The folk have no warriors to speak of, beyond a few watchmen and constables, and we far outnumber them. But we can't get in. We've tried every way. Storming the ramparts, throwing fire pots, whatever. The walls defeat us, and here we've been sitting for weeks, made to look like a pack of squabbling fools.'

" 'It seems easy enough to me,' I answer. 'Break down the gates, and there you are.'

"At this, he laughs in my face and tells me how they've tried that a dozen times. The gates are too strong, no way to breach them.

" 'In that case,' I answer, 'find a means to make the townsfolk themselves open the gates. Lure them out, then rush in as soon as the gates are ajar.'

" 'Do you think we haven't tried?' says Strong-of-Will. 'Useless. No, the trick's to get a few of my people inside and open the gates for us. And you, young fellow-me-lad, you tell me how to do that and, by heaven, I'll sail you home on one of our ships. We've got a fleet of them moored down there in the cove.'

" 'Consider it done,' say I, my mind running fast as a sea wind. And, after a little thought and calculation, I shaped a plan for him then and there. In sum: Use the timbers from one of his ships to build a great wooden jackass with a hollow belly big enough to hide a couple dozen warriors. First, I thought of a horse, but an ass struck me as being more insulting. Once the contraption's done, Strong-of-Will must proclaim loud enough for all the town to hear that the siege is over, everyone's going home, and here's a little gift expressing our opinion of you. Then, the warriors make a show of leaving, but stay lurking nearby.

" 'I'll miss my guess,' I tell Strong-of-Will, 'if the townsfolk don't haul the thing in as a prize of war and hold a triumphant celebration. At the right moment, your fellows climb out, unbar the gates, and the town's yours.'

"To keep a long tale short," Oudeis went on, "Strong-of-Will agreed. It took a good while, but I built that wooden jackass practically single-handedly. My plan worked exactly as I said it would. I'm sorry it did. That day still gives me nightmares.

"Strong-of-Will and his warriors got through the opened gates. I tagged along and saw it all. They burned that pretty little town to the ground, put every man to the sword; most of the women, too—the lucky ones. They found the runaway couple in the house of the lad's father. No more than half-grown youngsters, scared witless, huddled in a corner, clasping arms around each other. Strong-of-Will killed them both with one blow. He was bloody to the elbows, happy as if he was at a birthday party."

Oudeis waved a hand, as if brushing spiderwebs from his face. There was only the lap-lap of waves for a time, then he spoke again.

"Strong-of-Will was good as his word, I'll say that

much. He gave me a ship and crew. That's the last I saw of him."

"And so," said Lucian, "you got home."

Oudeis shook his head. "The ship foundered in a storm, all hands lost but me. I was washed ashore, who knows where, more dead than alive. From then on, I think I was a man accursed. The harder I tried to reach home, the farther I got from it. Oh, I could tell you how a one-eyed lunatic blacksmith wanted to chop me up for his dinner. And a dozen more disasters. But those are tales for another day."

"Do you believe a word of that?" whispered Fronto. "Dolphins, wooden jackasses, cannibal blacksmiths—"

"It's a great story, true or not." Lucian turned to Oudeis, who was staring into the water. "At the end, though, you must have found your way to Metara."

"Aye, after seven years," said the shipmaster. "As soon as I docked there, I went straight to Mirina's house. In I walk and there she is at her loom, winsome as ever. 'Mirina, my sweet,' I call out, 'I'm home!' She stares as if the eyes would pop out of her head. 'Why, honey-girl,' I say, 'don't you know me?'

" 'You?' she cries. 'Gone for three months, was it? And back seven years later?'

"And she throws a pot at my head, follows it up with other crockery, lays into me with a broom until I had to run for my life. I set sail that instant and never again showed my face in Metara. I took up the cargo trade once more, with hard years of little luck. But, at the end, the Lady of Wild Things gave me safe haven where you found me. Now, here I'm off to sea with a jackass aboard—which no doubt pays me back for building that wooden one."

"I've heard your account," came a voice from astern. "You're perfectly welcome to blame me for your troubles."

"Ops!" burst out Lucian as the scapegoat crawled from a hiding place amid the pile of provisions. "How did you manage—?"

"I brought him with me," said Joy-in-the-Dance.

19

The Voyages of Lucian

That's a harrowing tale, Oudeis." Joy-in-the-Dance untangled herself from the lines and netting. She winked at the shipmaster. "It gets better each time you tell it."

Lucian jumped up to embrace her; but, while his heart leaped, his feet slipped, and he promptly fell flat on his face as the vessel pitched on the rising waves. Oudeis cocked an eye at the girl, with as much fondness as astonishment.

"Is this the lass I used to bounce on my knee? Eh, little lady, I've not seen you since you went off to be a pythoness. But, here, here, what are you up to? I hadn't counted on two more passengers."

"Ops and I got aboard while you were all traipsing

back and forth loading things. It seemed the best way to save a lot of discussion."

"When your mother sent you away," began Lucian, picking himself up, "I thought I'd never see you again, never have a chance to tell you—"

"You truly are an Aiee-Ouch. You actually imagined I'd sit and twiddle my thumbs while you went sailing off? I told Ops he should stay behind, but he wouldn't hear of it."

"I felt it was my duty to be with all of you," said Ops. "So many things can go amiss on a sea voyage, I knew you'd need my services. Laurel-Crown and I have much to talk about and much to tell each other, but I promised I'd come back to her and she promised to wait for me."

"For you—for a pythoness—to disobey the Lady is bad enough," Lucian began. "Worse, because you did it on my account."

"There are going to be serious consequences," said Joy-in-the-Dance. "I know that. But I made my choice." Her face fell for an instant. "Do you wish I hadn't come?"

"I've heard all I want," broke in Oudeis. "Get those oars in the water," he ordered Lucian and Catch-a-Tick. "You, too, Oops, or whatever your name is. Hop to it."

"My good shipmaster," said Fronto, "you don't intend rowing all the way to Callista, do you?"

"Pull for shore," snapped Oudeis. "You, little lady, are going home."

"No, I'm not," said Joy-in-the-Dance. "Since I'll be punished anyway, I might as well be punished after I get back. And you, Oudeis, you know what it's like to be apart from someone."

Oudeis muttered and rubbed a big hand over his jaw. That instant, a brisk wind rose; the sail caught it and billowed taut. The waves heaved up and the little ship leaped ahead. Oudeis seized the rudder as the vessel sped seaward.

"It seems that Earth-Shaker's made the decision," said Joy-in-the-Dance. "He must have enjoyed that drink of wine."

By dawn, the shore lay far behind and they were in open sea, waves flashing in the early sunlight, the wind never slackening. The craft skimmed along faster than Lucian had imagined. With Joy-in-the-Dance beside him, the salt spray stinging his face, the vessel plunging up and down, he had never been in better spirits.

"Your mother couldn't tell me my best occupation," he said. "But here aboard—it's marvelous, it makes me wonder if—"

He broke off, sprang to his feet, and raced for the side. Fronto was already there, his neck stretched over the rail. Lucian followed the poet's example. The seafaring life, he decided, had its disadvantages.

He did not die. He was sorry about that, for he would have welcomed the relief. The endless tossing of the ship, the horizon tilting every which way, the blinding sun, the stink of pitch in his nostrils turned his stomach inside out and made his head reel. Joy-in-the-Dance, Ops, and even Catch-a-Tick were in fine fettle and hearty appetite, while Lucian spent much of his time hanging his head over the side. Fronto was in worse case. The miserable poet, his white-tipped nose gone pale green, sprawled on the deck, pitifully wheezing and groaning.

"Stop the boat," he wailed. "Heave-ho, or whatever you fellows do. I care no longer what becomes of me. I'll gladly stay a jackass forever. Only put me ashore."

"You'll find your sea legs," said Oudeis, unmoved. "Get up, you lubber, and stir yourself. Keep carrying on like that and, yes, by thunder, I'll maroon you on the first spit of land I come to."

"Don't talk about spit," whimpered Fronto.

Oudeis now handed out the straw hats from the pile of gear. To accommodate Fronto, he cut earholes in the crown of one and set it on the poet's head.

"It's quite becoming," remarked Joy-in-the-Dance. "You look very jaunty."

"Thank you," said Fronto. "I'll be sure to wear it when I jump overboard."

As for Lucian, the shipmaster gave him so many tasks that he had no time to be seasick. More frustrating, he and Joy-in-the-Dance stood separate watches, and he found no right moment for speaking his heart to her. He cheered himself by turning his thoughts to the shipmaster's tale.

"What a storyteller Oudeis is," he said to Fronto, who had recovered enough to sit up on his haunches. Lucian shook his head in admiration. "I hope he'll tell us more of his tales."

"He's one of the best I've heard," said Fronto, "but that wooden jackass could stand a little improvement. I understand why he used an ass. Even so, I'd change it to a horse. Though I hate to admit it, a jackass doesn't have the same elegance, that certain flair. And another thing: Strong-of-Will and his men were a grubby lot of provincials. That doesn't exactly pluck at the imagination."

"You could change that, too," Lucian suggested. "You could make his army bigger, with, say, a thousand ships. And the town bigger, with huge, high walls, topless towers. And have the bravest townsmen come out and do mortal combat with Strong-of-Will's people. You know, slashing each other with swords, the kind of thing you expected from the *lyrikos*. Maybe on horseback—"

"Why, my boy, I believe you're beginning to see how

it's done. Yes, of course. Mighty warriors with plumed helmets, powerful thews, girded loins, and all that. An array of proud and noble heroes—"

"Bilge," said Oudeis, passing by. "I've seen many a brawl and no heroes in any. Unless you count some wretch knifed in the belly, holding his guts in his hands and bawling for his mamma. Nobility? Not a speck."

"Even so," said Lucian, "I'd think you'd need glorious heroes in a tale for people to admire and praise and be inspired to act like them."

"Eh, lad, you may be right." Oudeis shrugged. "Otherwise, who'd ever want to go fighting?"

A few days out, after taking stock of the dwindling stores, Oudeis declared that he would have to make for the nearest port. He had sighted land and what looked like a harbor off the starboard bow.

"I don't know the place. There's more islands in these waters than even I've seen. I wanted to wait and tie up in a snug little place where I'm well known, but I can't risk it. We're too low on supplies. So, I'm putting in as quick as I can."

"By all means!" cried Fronto. "For mercy's sake, let me stand on dry land until my stomach and I are friends again. Don't tell me about getting my sea legs. You forget I have four of them to deal with."

As Oudeis set a landward course, the harbor came into better view. Fishing boats and a long ship, its black sail reefed, were at the wharves. Lucian made out a pleasant-looking, unwalled town, some tree-lined avenues, and a large, stone building overlooking all. Oudeis lowered the sail and ordered his crew to the oars. Fronto clambered to the prow and stood like a long-eared figurehead.

"They've seen us. They're waving," he called. "Some of them have bunches of flowers. A happy welcome, indeed. Faster! Pull hard on those oars."

With Fronto urging more effort, and Oudeis skillfully steering past the harbor bar, the ship glided into port and slid gently to an open pier. Some of the townsfolk ran to catch the line that Oudeis cast over the side. Others set up a gangplank and beckoned the visitors to step ashore.

"Keep your mouth shut. Say nothing," Lucian warned as Fronto, with a joyful hee-haw, clambered onto the dock, Catch-a-Tick at his heels. Having secured his ship, Oudeis strode after Lucian, Joy-in-the-Dance, and Ops. A crowd had gathered, smiling and offering flowers to the newcomers.

"I don't quite catch what they're talking about," said Joy-in-the-Dance. "The language is a little bit of Mother Tongue but mostly something else. The island's Tauros —that's what it sounds like. I'm not sure, but they seem to think we've come to collect some kind of tribute."

"I'll sort it out," said Oudeis. "Seafarers understand each other."

By this time, an escort of warriors in helmets and breastplates had pressed through the crowd and pointed up toward the town. "They want us to see their king," said Joy-in-the-Dance. "So I gather, anyway. His name's Bolynthos."

"I look forward to the opportunity," Fronto said under his breath. "As a poet, I was never invited to meet royalty."

"Nor will you meet any this time," said Oudeis. "You stay with me. A palace is no place for an ass; not the four-legged kind, at any rate. I'll need you to help load provisions."

"The Bull Court?" Joy-in-the-Dance murmured to Lucian as the warriors formed ranks around them. "Is that what they're saying?"

The escort marched them along an avenue lined with onlookers, cheering and tossing flower petals. The building that Lucian had sighted from offshore—the royal palace, he supposed—bulked larger than it had first appeared. Of heavy stone slabs, it was flat roofed, almost windowless. Adjoining it rose a circular structure, a sort of amphitheater with arched entryways. Beyond the palace gates, at the end of a flagstoned passage, attendants flung open bronze portals to an audience chamber. Rows of torches blazed, a sickly sweet aroma of incense hung in the air. On a throne of ornately carved wood, a powerfully built man sprawled lazily. A purple cloak was draped over his shoulders, a gem-studded leather collar circled his thick neck. For a moment, he observed the arrivals with vague interest, then made an offhand gesture for them to approach.

"King Bolynthos?" Joy-in-the-Dance courteously began in Mother Tongue. "We thank you for your welcome and—"

"Not asked to speak," the king interrupted, in a rough version of Mother Tongue. He had the dark brown eyes of an ox and they seemed too large for their sockets. His long black hair had been curled into ringlets around a wide and bulging brow. He turned his massive head toward Lucian. "This man answers."

"This woman answers." Joy-in-the-Dance said in Mother Tongue. "I am the one who speaks for all of us."

"Silence!" The king's eyes suddenly widened to show white all around, and dark blood rushed to his face. Just as quickly, his features relaxed into a crooked smile. "You dance well for me, that is all." He returned to Lucian. "Say on."

Lucian glanced at Joy-in-the-Dance, who shrugged

and translated the king's words. He began slowly, "We come from Arkadia, most of us. We have stopped here to buy—"

Bolynthos scowled and waved a hand laden with bracelets and rings. "Arkadia? I know of Arkadia. Beyond the sea. The rest—I cannot understand your tongue. Let the woman address the Bull King."

"Your Majesty," said Joy-in-the-Dance, holding down her annoyance, "we stopped for food and water. We must keep on our way. We seek no tribute from you."

"From me?" Bolynthos flung back his head and bellowed with laughter. "I do not give. You give."

"There's a misunderstanding," said Joy-in-the-Dance. "We have no tribute."

"You do," said Bolynthos. "All of you. Were you not told? The tribute is—your lives."

"That," said Joy-in-the-Dance, "is a very serious misunderstanding."

20

Asterion

For Lucian, a number of daring possibilities sprang to mind: flinging himself bodily on the king, who had folded his arms and was grimly smiling at his captives; or snatching a sword from one of the guards; or taking hold of Joy-in-the-Dance and dashing headlong from the audience chamber; or signaling Ops to join him in fighting off the warriors while the girl and Catch-a-Tick made their escape. He did, as it turned out, none of these.

In fact, before he could weigh the advantages and disadvantages of his choices, he was already being hauled away by the guards and punched or kicked when he struggled and tried to drag his heels; what he mostly did was to shout indignant protests and colorful threats. It took him a few moments to realize that Joy-in-the-Dance was no longer with him.

By then, he was being frog-marched down one passageway after the other, with so many twists and turns, so many dark galleries, ramps, flights of stone steps going up and down that he entirely lost his bearings. He had not the vaguest notion where he was or, even if he could break loose, how to find his way out.

Ops kept a cautious but alert silence. Catch-a-Tick pranced along, not the least dismayed.

"Aiee-Ouch, that was a clever trick to get us out of the throne room," he whispered. "Who'd have thought of letting them drag us off?" When Lucian only shook his head, Catch-a-Tick gave a knowing wink. "Right. Not a word. They might overhear us."

Lucian, more than half out of his wits over the unknown fate of Joy-in-the-Dance, was too distressed to correct the boy's admiring view. Also, he was dazzled a moment by sudden light after so many dim corridors; for his captors now thrust their prisoners into a large stone chamber, where afternoon sun poured through a long, narrow grating in the far wall. Blinking in the glare, he first made out a huddle of shadows: some dozen men in dirty tunics, in coarse shirts, or stripped to the waist. Catch-a-Tick ran to peer through the bars. Ops, hands on hips, stood observing appraisingly as these captives got to their feet and gathered around the newcomers, talking all at once.

"I don't know what you're saying," Lucian broke in, recognizing only a word here and there. "Does no one speak Arkadian?"

"I do." A tall, reddish-haired young man approached, and the others drew aside to let him pass. "Why are you here? Bolynthos has no claim on Arkadia."

After Lucian explained that they had merely stopped to take on food and water, Asterion, as he named himself, smiled bitterly. "A costly mistake. Alas that you ever set foot on Tauros. This is the time when Bolynthos receives his tribute."

Asterion gestured toward his companions. "Each year, he demands youths and maidens from the king of Naxos. The girl you spoke of is no doubt with our women, penned up as we are. You will surely see her again: tomorrow, at the bull dance. I am sorry."

"I don't understand any of this," replied Lucian. "How could we have known? Everyone seemed friendly. They were throwing flowers at us."

"Of course," said Asterion, "they were overjoyed to see you. On the voyage from our island, two of our company sickened and died; two others, in despair, threw themselves overboard. Thus, the full tribute is lacking. When that happens, Bolynthos is too impatient to await replacements from Naxos. He chooses victims from his own people. Small wonder you were so happily welcomed. Your unlucky arrival spared some Taurians their lives. As long as he has victims enough to satisfy him, Bolynthos cares not where they come from. You are here, you will serve the purpose."

"I've seen goats dance." Catch-a-Tick, all ears, came to join his elders. "But—bulls? They're so stupid and heavy-footed. Dance? What a sight!"

"And one you shall see for yourself," Asterion said. "Those who live through it are, by rule, set free. But no victim has ever survived to claim that right. Yes, it is a dance—a dance of death."

"The king of Tauros is a beast," said Lucian, "and his people no better, if they take pleasure in bloodshed."

"The people are sick of it," Asterion replied. "They come to watch because they fear to do otherwise. Those who show no stomach for the sport could find themselves ordered into the arena. But unless all rise as one against Bolynthos, the killing will go on."

"What about the king of Naxos?" said Lucian. "If he knows what happens to his people, why does he keep sending them?"

"He has little choice," Asterion said. "The yearly tribute began when Bolynthos came to the throne. At that time, he sent an ambassador to us, to discuss trade, treaties, and such affairs of state. There was a quarrel, tempers rose; a rash, ill-considered blow, and the ambassador was slain. This was a blood crime of gravest consequence. The person of an ambassador is sacred, inviolate. As was his right, Bolynthos demanded retribution: not in goods or money, but in lives. He required a group of young men and maidens to be sent him as sacrifice. We could not refuse.

"And so it was done. This should have washed clean our blood guilt, yet Bolynthos remained unsatisfied. Each year, he demanded yet another tribute, and another. He took pleasure in their death. When we protested, he warned that he had ships and warriors enough to invade Naxos and burn it to the ground.

"The king bowed to his will, reckoning the sacrifice of a few would safeguard the lives of many. Every year, victims were chosen by casting lots. But now, in this first season of my manhood, I resolved to end this slaughter. I joined the group ready to set sail, despite my father's pleading. As his son, I was exempt—"

"Wait a moment," said Lucian. "You didn't have to take your chances when the lots were cast?"

"Did I not make it clear? My father is the king. I am Asterion, prince of Naxos."

Ops, listening closely and silently during this, now spoke up. "You chose nobly, Lord Prince," he said, "but if your goal was to save your people and end the tribute, allow me to ask—with all respect—how have you gone about doing it? What plan have you shaped?"

"None," replied Asterion, "because none is possible. When I sailed from Naxos, I had a dozen schemes in mind. Now that I have seen for myself, my plans turned out to be useless fantasies."

Ops frowned. "Lord Prince, you are a leader of your people, are you not? Would you have me believe you've done nothing? Let me point out—again, with all respect—that if nothing is possible, you have nothing to lose. Even the most desperate action is better than none at all."

Ops had spoken in a tone Lucian had never heard before. Looking at the scapegoat now, he realized that Ops had changed since Mount Panthea. His voice was calm but firm, his bearing showed an authority Lucian had not suspected. He suddenly remembered that Ops himself had been a chieftain.

"I said you had done nothing," Ops went on. "I was wrong. You have done something. You have waited to be killed."

Asterion's chin went up. His voice was low and cold. "How dare you rebuke me? As I cannot save my people, the best I can do is die with them. Who are you to tell me otherwise? You know nothing of what happens here. You speak from ignorance."

Asterion took a pace closer to Ops and thrust his face at him. "When you have seen what we have seen, then will you have the right to reproach me. Escape? None, save into the bullring. Beyond this chamber, we would be lost in the passageways. Bolynthos had them built for that purpose. The maze is a better warden than any guard. I know this. Do not take me for a fool, let alone a weakling. I and some of my companions burst out once when the guards came to feed us.

"They made no attempt to stop us. They watched, and laughed; and after we had wandered blindly, they fetched us back at their leisure. In the bullring, there is no way to flee. Only the dead leave it. Each morning, they herd us there and we wait our time to face the bulls.

"On our first day," Asterion went on, his voice faltering an instant, "Bolynthos ordered out three of our maidens, one of them little more than a child. They were nimble. Yes, and clever, too. They did not cling to one another, cowering in fright, but ran in different directions to confuse and distract the bull.

"They were very brave. I was proud of them, and even thought they might live out the day. But their efforts only exhausted them. They tired long before the bull did.

One lost her footing, stumbled, and fell. The creature was upon her within the blink of an eye.

"The other two—it was only a matter of time." Asterion strained to keep his voice under control, but his eyes darted back and forth. "Afterward, the attendants spread fresh sand where it was needed, and raked it smooth. They like to keep the arena tidy.

"And thus it has gone, day after day, always much the same. Now," said Asterion between his teeth, "perhaps you will be kind enough to instruct me in my proper duties, and point out to me what I should do. I will be most interested in your suggestions."

"Indeed, I spoke from ignorance," murmured Ops. "I well understand your fear—"

Asterion gave a bitter laugh. "Fear? We have gone past the limits of fear. Here, we eat and drink it, and finally grow bored with it. I no longer pray for courage. I pray for madness. Sanity becomes too heavy a burden."

"You are still their prince," Ops replied. "It is a burden you must carry."

"I shall gladly lay it down."

Asterion turned away and strode to a corner of the chamber.

"Don't you worry, Asterion," called Catch-a-Tick, swaggering up and down and pointing to Lucian. "Here's the greatest hero in Arkadia. Lucian Aiee-Ouch, mighty warrior, lord of wolves and everything else you'd care to mention. Yes, and I also happen to be the son of a king. I'm Goat Prince Catch-a-Tick, friend of the hero. Everything will be fine. We have a plan—"

"Be quiet," Lucian ordered.

"I forgot. Sorry," said Catch-a-Tick. "You wanted to keep it mum." He closed his mouth tightly and trotted over to Ops, who had gone to Asterion's side.

Lucian went to the grating and stared out at the empty arena. He could not clear his head of Asterion's words. He seemed to hear endlessly echoing screams, to smell fresh blood and the animal reek from the bull pens. He could not guess where Joy-in-the-Dance had been locked up. For all he knew, her cell could be far across the stretch of sand or next to his own. He called out, but no answer came.

He stood some while as the shadow that covered half the arena crept to the farthest tiers of benches and all lay in darkness. He sank down, at last, and put his head in his hands. Catch-a-Tick came and sat beside him, yawning.

"Now you can tell me, just between us," the boy whispered. "You've got it all thought out, haven't you?"

"I don't know what you're talking about."

"The plan! It's working, isn't it? You got us into the same cell as those Naxians. That was the cleverest yet.

Asterion—I hope I didn't make him feel second-rate."
Catch-a-Tick yawned still more widely and leaned heavily against the wall. "He's not much of a prince. And he's no kind of hero at all."

"Neither am I," Lucian said firmly. "I want you to stop this nonsense. Half of what I told you I made up, and you made up the other half. There weren't any meat cleavers. I never led any wolves. Most of the time, I was afraid they'd bite me. Warrior? I got smacked on the head with the flat of a sword. That's all. Nothing but stories and stories and stories. I don't have a plan. I never did. I just want to crawl in a hole somewhere and hide. Do you understand what I'm telling you?"

The boy said nothing. Lucian raised his head and glanced at him. A happy smile on his face, Catch-a-Tick was fast asleep.

21

The Bull Dance

It was a busy morning. Asterion and his companions had been up early, belting tunics, lacing sandals, rubbing arms and legs with oil, as if getting ready for a day of sport. When Lucian asked why they bothered with such careful preparations, Asterion shrugged and said that it gave them something to occupy their minds.

Lucian, in his own way, had been doing much the same, turning his thoughts to Joy-in-the-Dance, Fronto, and Oudeis. He was sure that Oudeis had already learned of their plight. If the shipmaster was as clever as he claimed to be, he would have understood that he could do nothing to help. His only practical choice would be to set sail as quickly as possible. Fronto, at least, would be on his way to Callista.

He still had no idea where Joy-in-the-Dance was being held. Asterion pointed toward a line of shoulder-high wooden barriers on the far side of the arena. Like the men, the women would be taken behind them to wait until ordered into the ring.

"For you and your friends," Asterion added, "there is little advice I can give. Never turn your back on the bull. Stay as far from the beast as you can. Apart from that, it becomes a highly personal matter between you and the bull."

Soon afterward, guards came to lead the victims through a tunnel that opened onto the arena. There was some joking back and forth, and some easy conversation. The guards, good-natured fellows, were trying to keep the business from turning too grim.

Lucian spoke closely with Ops. "Asterion says to keep our distance from the bull. He should know, but I can't help wondering if that's best. I had an idea—"

"I knew it!" cried Catch-a-Tick. "You're working on your plan. Tell me what I do."

"What you do is stay away from us. I don't want you anywhere close to Ops and me."

"I don't think much of that," said Catch-a-Tick.

"Never mind. Just do as I say," Lucian ordered and finished his talk with Ops out of the boy's hearing.

The tunnel ended abruptly at the edge of the arena.

The sudden burst of light, the yellow sand under the glaring sun dazzled him. He shaded his eyes to look across the amphitheater. He thought he saw a hand waving and raised his own in answer. Most of the benches were filled, spectators still picked their way to the upper tiers. On a stone platform at the edge of the ring, Bolynthos sat under a fringed canopy. In full regalia, jewels glittering, he cradled a long-handled, double-headed ax and a scepter topped by golden horns. His eyes were bulging and rolling, his face flushed. He motioned with his head. Trumpets blared, someone began shouting an announcement Lucian could not understand.

"You Arkadians lead off," Asterion explained. "Step out boldly. If you try to hold back, it will only go worse for you. Lucian Aiee-Ouch, whoever you are, I wish you well. I trust you are the hero your young friend believes you to be."

The prince of Naxos turned to Ops. "You were right to rebuke me. For that, I thank you. I had almost forgotten I was a prince. When my turn comes, I hope I shall behave like one. Farewell."

Before Lucian could stop him, Catch-a-Tick darted through the gap between the barriers and trotted to the middle of the arena, where he put his hands on his hips and grinned around impudently. No cheers or shouts came from the spectators, only a long, sighing murmur;

then, silence as the gates at the far end flung open. Bolynthos leaned forward. The bull had come into the arena.

The creature no doubt had been deliberately goaded and tormented to liven him up, for he burst out of the gate at full speed, bellowing, tossing his horns, galloping around the ring. He was very angry. He was very large.

Lucian stared, rooted to the spot. His plan had been simple and logical. As he explained it to Ops, instead of keeping their distance and wasting their strength avoiding the creature, they would go straight at the bull, each grip one of the horns and hang on to it. Thus, they needed only keep hold and do nothing more. The bull would have to tire before they did.

As he had thought about it in the cell, the idea seemed excellent. He wondered why it had never occurred to Asterion. Now that he was actually in the arena, he understood. He had never imagined the animal to be quite so huge and powerful. In fact, he had never seen a bull face-to-face. He had, he suspected, misjudged the reality of the situation. All things considered, taking to his heels seemed the more attractive course. But as in a nightmare, he could not force his legs to move.

The bull, meantime, had stopped galloping aimlessly and cast about for some object on which to vent his rage. Ops glanced at Lucian, motioned with his head, and began cautiously approaching the animal. Lucian finally extorted some grudging obedience from his legs, but they felt made of lead as he plodded over the sand. It was important, he realized, to grasp the horns before the creature charged.

The bull had a different plan in mind. Lucian had gone less than halfway when the creature drew into himself, gathering his force, then bolted forward, head lowered, faster than Lucian believed possible. Ops leaped to one side, Lucian to the other, as the bull slewed around to charge again.

Catch-a-Tick, so far, had obeyed Lucian's orders to stay away; but now, legs pumping, the boy shot across the ring straight for the bull. The animal paused a moment, as if considering what to do about this new arrival. Without breaking stride, whooping and crowing, Catch-a-Tick vaulted onto the creature's back. The bull did not like this. He bucked and reared, flinging the boy into the air. Catch-a-Tick landed with both feet on the massive shoulders. Turning his attention from Lucian and Ops, the bull strove to shake off what he must have judged to be some oversized and exasperating fly, heaving and twisting, bellowing at the top of his lungs. Each time Catch-a-Tick was tossed aloft, he nimbly regained his perch on the bull's back or hindquarters and, once, even managed to do a somersault in midair.

Seeing the bull preoccupied with Catch-a-Tick, who had begun a jaunty little dance up and down the creature's spine, Lucian and Ops darted ahead, each seizing one of the curved horns. Lucian feared his arms might tear loose from their sockets, but he clung with all his strength. Ops, little by little, was wrestling the shaggy head closer to the sand. From the tail of his eye, Lucian glimpsed a slender shape speeding from the women's barrier.

"Stop that!" cried Joy-in-the-Dance. "You're annoying the poor thing."

She stepped to the bull and laid a hand between the horns, murmuring something Lucian could not understand. The animal left off struggling and blinked at her. "Let go, Aiee-Ouch. You, too, Ops. Catch-a-Tick, come down from there."

The girl stroked the hairy ears, all the while whispering and half singing. This was not only the first time Lucian had seen a bull, it was also the first time he had seen one smile. The crowd was cheering and shouting. The bull trotted to the edge of the arena, folded his legs, and lay down. The crowd started a rhythmic chanting and clapping.

"They want us set free," Joy-in-the-Dance explained while Catch-a-Tick bowed and capered. "Bolynthos won't dare refuse. Oh—now they're saying that—"

She broke off. Ignoring the swelling tide of voices, the king had jumped to his feet. He gestured for a new bull to be sent in. The gate remained shut. The crowd roared all the louder. Bolynthos, cheeks twisting and twitching, sprang from the platform. Brandishing the double ax, he strode toward Joy-in-the-Dance.

The girl calmly pointed her outspread hands at him. "Here, look. Why are you holding that serpent? It's enormous! See, it's coiling around your arm. It's going to strike. Those fangs—look at them, they're deadly poison. Quick, quick, get rid of the horrible thing."

Bolynthos stopped in his tracks, gaping. He stared at the ax, struggled with the handle as if it were indeed coiling around him. With a shriek, he threw down the weapon.

"Run, you three," ordered Joy-in-the-Dance. "I can't hold his mind much longer."

"Bolynthos!"

Asterion had sprinted from behind the barrier, his companions at his heels. Bolynthos shook himself, as if suddenly waking. He thrust aside Joy-in-the-Dance and lurched to recover the ax. Asterion snatched it and sprang away. The king's hand went to the sword at his belt. Asterion swung the ax like a man felling a tree. Bolynthos grunted and dropped to one knee. Asterion struck again.

Lucian did not look back at what Asterion was doing. He could barely keep his heaving stomach where it belonged as he ran with Joy-in-the-Dance to the arcade circling the arena. Before they reached it, the gate of the bull pens opened. Lucian called a warning. Joy-in-the-Dance halted to face another onslaught.

Fronto trotted out. He stopped a moment, blinking in the sunlight. As the cheers rose louder, the poet bent a foreleg and bobbed his head in acknowledgment, then galloped to Lucian's side. Oudeis and a crowd of seafaring men pressed into the arena after him.

"That was a nice round of applause they gave me," said Fronto. "Who's the fellow with the ax?"

"Never mind that now," said Lucian while Oudeis and his comrades hustled them unchallenged past the bull pens and out of the amphitheater.

The streets lay empty; nearly all the townspeople were still at the arena. Lucian hurried to follow the shipmaster toward the waterfront.

"By luck, I ran into some of my old shipmates," Oudeis said. "I found out quick enough what was going on, and they were glad to give me a hand. They're not fond of Bolynthos. Nobody is. I'm sorry it took us so long. We couldn't risk getting lost in those passageways, so we had to wait and follow the crowd into the arena."

Catch-a-Tick, skipping beside Lucian, kept recounting the events to Fronto. "Aiee-Ouch planned the whole thing. He had it all worked out from the first. Oudeis didn't need to bother rescuing us."

"I wish I'd been able to recite a paean of victory," said Fronto. "I don't usually find such a large and enthusiastic audience."

"No more tribute, no more victims," Lucian said to Joy-in-the-Dance. "What a relief for his father and the whole kingdom when Asterion brings home the good news. You saved us all when you made Bolynthos see the snake."

"I didn't make him," the girl corrected. "I only suggested."

"Whatever you did," said Lucian, with a shudder, "it felt like some of it rubbed off on me. For a moment, I thought I really saw the ax coiling around him. But why didn't Bolynthos spare our lives? That's what the crowd wanted. He must have gone mad, if he wasn't mad in the first place."

"I didn't have a chance to explain then," said Joy-in-the-Dance, "but there was something more. The crowd started shouting for him to give up his throne or they'd take it away from him. That was enough to put him in a fine rage. What sent him over the edge—well, you see, they not only wanted to get rid of him, they also wanted me to be queen of Tauros."

22

Earth-Shaker's Chickens

ad, that's a tale to match any of mine," said Oudeis
as the boat sped over calm waters and the island
dropped from sight. The shipmaster had been listening
with rapt attention, hanging on every word while Lucian
gave his account of all that had befallen them—and
Catch-a-Tick kept interrupting to add details of his own
part in it.

"Well told, my boy," said Fronto, nodding approval.
"Satisfyingly bloodcurdling but, perhaps, needing a touch
of something to relieve the grimness and lighten it up a
bit. Next time you tell it, you might work in some tender
moments. To warm the heart and bring a tear to the eye.
The only thing more touching than lovers separated is

lovers reunited. You could use those twisting passageways to better effect, as well. What I'd suggest—"

"Stow all that! Take the tiller!" Oudeis shouted to
Ops. The shipmaster had gone pale beneath his tan.
"Blast me for a fool! I've been listening to that yarn spinning as if nothing else mattered in the world." He rum-
maged in the cargo and pulled out the wineskin. "It
slipped my mind. A drink for Earth-Shaker."

"Come now, Oudeis, be reasonable," said Fronto.
"You did your duty by him when we sailed from Mount
Panthea. Don't waste wine that could be put to other,
some might say more discriminating, use."

"A lot you know, you landlubber." Oudeis, much agitated, upended the wineskin and poured its contents
over the side. "Whenever I've neglected Earth-Shaker—
and it hasn't been often—there's trouble. There, that's
the best I can do. I hope it's not too late."

"I'd say the old fellow's been doing well for us,"
Fronto said confidently. "We couldn't ask for calmer
seas, a better breeze, or a clearer sky."

"What do you call that, eh?" Oudeis pointed upward.
"It wasn't there a moment ago." He squinted at the gray-
ish cloud high overhead, so distant it seemed no bigger
than a fist.

"Hardly worth getting upset," said Fronto.

"You think not?" snapped Oudeis. "Stick to poetry, jackass, and don't teach me about weather." Taking the tiller from Ops, the shipmaster ordered his passengers to lash down the cargo. Sniffing the wind, keeping an eye on the cloud, he held the vessel steadily on course.

"It's my fault," Lucian said to Fronto. "I shouldn't have talked so much. Going on about what happened— I made him forget his gift to Earth-Shaker."

"Oh, you got his attention," said Fronto. "From a yarn spinner like Oudeis, that's a high compliment. It's not often that one storyteller bothers listening to another.

"Here's something that's occurred to me," Fronto went on. "The Lady couldn't tell you what occupation to follow. But I can. I've been observing you, my boy. I have the answer."

"Then you've found it sooner than I have," Lucian said. "What is it?"

"Storytelling, what else?" declared Fronto. "You have the knack for it. Of that, I'm certain. A little practice and you'll come along nicely."

"No, I'm afraid not," Lucian said, with a shadow of regret. "That takes more skill than I'll ever have."

"Nonsense," Fronto insisted. "You're already a storyteller without even knowing it. Indeed, nothing would please me more, and I'd be proud to call you a colleague. You think over what I'm saying—Haw! Haw!"

Fronto choked and rolled his eyes in alarm. "What was that? I didn't mean to say it. That haw-haw slipped out by itself. That's pure jackass, not me at all.

"The Lady warned me," Fronto went on, in mounting panic, "I'd start losing my speech and be more and more a donkey. It's happening already? Dear boy, this is dreadful."

"You're speaking clearly as ever. You're fine," Lucian hastily assured him, trying to hide his own sudden alarm. "Don't upset yourself. It might—it might have been something you ate."

"I haw—I hope—you're right," Fronto said unhappily. "Yes, perhaps only a transitory hiccup."

Putting all thoughts of Fronto's advice out of his mind, Lucian hurried to Joy-in-the-Dance, who had finished knotting a rope around the kegs and jars. The girl frowned when Lucian told her what had so distressed the poet.

"That's not a good sign," she said. "My mother told us he had time enough to get to the island, but she didn't count on our getting thrown into a bullring."

With Lucian, she went to Oudeis, who was glumly scanning the horizon. "How much longer to Callista?"

"Ask Earth-Shaker. It's more up to him now than to me."

"We've a good strong wind," put in Lucian. "That should help."

"Too strong, and it's fishtailing all around. I can barely hold course. I don't like it. And I don't like—them."

Oudeis gestured astern. A flock of birds had appeared, following the wake of the vessel. Lucian shaded his eyes. The birds were sleek and slender, black with a flash of white; their widespread, sharply curved wings bore them swiftly, ever closer.

"Earth-Shaker's chickens, we call them." Oudeis grimaced. "Or wave walkers."

"We call them Lady's hens," said Joy-in-the-Dance. "They're petrels, they won't harm us."

"Storm birds, by any name. The bigger the flock, the bigger the blow."

"They follow storms, they don't cause them."

"It comes to the same. Shoo, shoo!" Oudeis shouted and flailed an arm as if he were, indeed, chasing off invading chickens.

Even as Lucian watched, the waves turned choppy and rose higher. The wind freshened; within moments, the vessel heaved and shuddered. Oudeis laid all his strength of arm on the tiller.

The little fist-shaped cloud had lengthened into a gigantic hand, its twisted fingers clutched the darkening sky. The craft shot ahead like an arrow from a bow, tossed so high that it seemed to fly through the air.

Fronto, knocked off his legs, braying in terror, went skittering across the deck. Catch-a-Tick jumped up and down, gleefully whooping.

Lightning clawed the sky. A thunderclap set Lucian's head ringing. The shock staggered him; he felt as if the air had been sucked out of his lungs. The kegs and jars had begun jolting free of their lashings.

Oudeis bellowed for Ops to lend a hand. "The lines are fouled. I can't lower the sail. It has to come down, or the gale's going to smash us into kindling." He spat furiously. "No use. To the masthead! Cut those lines or we'll all go visiting Earth-Shaker."

Still dazed, Lucian stared around. Oudeis shook his fist at him. "I'm talking to you, idiot. Get aloft. Snap to it."

"Me?"

"Who else, you lubber? I need Ops to help me hold the tiller. I'm your only navigator. The goat-boy and the jackass can't do it. I'll not risk the little lady's neck. That leaves you."

"I appreciate your reasoning," said Lucian.

"Then do, you lump-head!" Oudeis snatched a knife from his belt and tossed it to Lucian, who stumbled toward the mast. Blade clenched between his teeth, he took hold of the rigging and tried to persuade himself it was not much worse than the tree he once climbed.

"There goes Aiee-Ouch!" Catch-a-Tick jigged up and down and clapped his hands. "Who but Aiee-Ouch would dare do that!"

The swaying mast towered above him. Hand over hand, he inched his way upward. The vessel tilted, nearly capsizing. He hung on, dangling from the lines as the craft righted itself. The sky split, rain began sheeting down. His foot caught in one of the lines, he kicked loose and climbed higher. A line had tangled around the yard-arm. He slashed at the wet knots. The line frayed, then parted with a snap. The sail billowed free as the mast shuddered, groaned, and toppled into the web of rigging. Lucian jumped clear. The craft spun around and flung him against the railing. The tiller had shattered. Oudeis was shouting something. With the wind howling in his ears, Lucian heard none of it; nor did he hear the ship scream as the hull ripped apart.

❧

He knew he was alive because he was choking and coughing. He knew he was on land because he was flat on his stomach with gritty sand on his face and in his eyes. He rolled over and blinked. It was a clear and beautiful morning.

"Hullo, Aiee-Ouch." Joy-in-the-Dance was on one side of him, Ops and Oudeis on the other. "You must have swallowed half the ocean, but we've squeezed most of it out of you."

"I knew my services would be needed," said Ops as Lucian sat up, relieved to find the amulet still around his neck; the pouch, with the sling and firestones, had likewise survived the battering.

"You cut down the sail at just the right time," said Catch-a-Tick, "so the boat smashed on those rocks. Oudeis says if we'd been farther from land, we'd have drowned. Fronto let me ride on his back when he waded ashore."

The poet himself was standing stiff-legged, wheezing and snuffling. "Difficult to express adequate joy that we're all alive," he said in a husky voice. "Either I've caught cold or it's getting harder to talk. Not that it matters. One way or another, I'm doomed."

"Belay that maundering," ordered Oudeis. "Just be grateful we slipped through Earth-Shaker's fingers." He glanced seaward, shaking his head. "My little ship, my brave little ship, gone to splinters, not enough of her left to cobble a raft."

"Farewell, Callista," groaned Fronto. "I'll be a jackass for certain."

"I said I'll take you there," declared Oudeis, "and so I will."

"Perhaps you're thinking of building wings," remarked Fronto, "so we can flap our way off this island."

"What island?" retorted Oudeis. "I've been doing some calculations. As I reckon it, counting from the time we were blown off course, we're not on an island. We're on the south coast of Arkadia."

"Arkadia?" Lucian jumped to his feet. "Last place in the world we want to be!"

"Here we are, no matter," said Oudeis, "and we'll have to make the best of it. So, we're going to walk. No use following the shoreline. There aren't many folk in these parts. Maybe a fishing village or two. But a fishing boat won't do for a voyage to Callista. We need a good seaworthy craft. I know how to get one.

"We head inland," he went on. "It would take too long to go by way of the coast. We go due north awhile, then turn seaward. In less than a week, we'll reach Metara."

"Oudeis, I don't dare set foot in Metara," said Lucian. "If anyone from the palace sees me, if Calchas and Phobos find out I'm there, it's worth my life."

"We have no other choice," Oudeis said. "We won't go into the town. We head straight for the harbor, where the merchant vessels put in. It's a sure thing I'll find some old shipmates to help us. You have the Lady's amulet? Good. There's many a shipmaster owes her a favor. We'll have a deck under our feet and be off to Callista quick as you can whistle. I'll sail with you, to be certain all goes handsomely."

Oudeis ordered them to scavenge among the broken timbers and other flotsam that had washed ashore. The search yielded little: a small keg of dried fish, a cook pot, and Fronto's straw hat. With these, and a couple of cloaks, Oudeis was satisfied, declaring they could add to their provisions along the way.

"I'll tell you right now," said Oudeis, setting off over the sand dunes and up to the bluffs overlooking the coast, "this is my last voyage. Dry land for the rest of my days. No more touch-and-go with Earth-Shaker. Once I'm back from Callista, by thunder, I'll take an oar and walk inland. When someone asks, 'What's that strange-looking piece of wood?'—there's where I'll settle."

Oudeis proved as skillful a pilot on land as on sea; only Joy-in-the-Dance could match him in choosing the easiest paths leading steadily north. Their first day, as they crossed the windswept moorlands beyond the coast, Lucian observed a solitary bird high in the clouds.

"An eagle," said Joy-in-the-Dance as the bird glided closer, hovering on outspread, golden wings. "Did my mother send it to watch over us?"

For all her efforts to lure it down, the eagle came no nearer. Nevertheless, during the following days, it was seldom out of sight.

The moorlands gave way to richer vegetation; the trees became denser, the undergrowth heavier. Catch-a-Tick, proud to show off his skill, taught Lucian how to strike sparks from the firestones. With the boy's instruction, Lucian was soon able to build a cook fire; and Joy-in-the-Dance was always quick to find roots and berries to eke out their scanty meals.

Late one afternoon, when they halted for the day, Lucian spoke apart with her. "Do you remember the night of the dancing? Something your father said to me. And I keep thinking—when your mother sent me away. I've been wanting to tell you—"

"Be quiet, Aiee-Ouch."

"But I want you to know—"

"Hush. Somebody's in the bushes and it isn't one of us."

The girl motioned for Ops and Oudeis. That moment, a bulky figure lurched from the undergrowth. The man's garments hung in tatters, his hair and beard so matted and his face so begrimed that Lucian hardly recognized him.

It was King Bromios.

23

A King in Rags

Lucian jumped to his feet. "Your Majesty—"

"Stand away!" Bromios shoved him aside and lunged for the cook pot. Though the vessel had been simmering over the fire, he snatched it up, paying no mind to his burned fingers, and began scooping out the contents and cramming the morsels into his mouth as fast as he could.

"Here, you, that's our food." Catch-a-Tick started toward Bromios, who held one arm protectively over the pot and fended off the boy with the other.

"Let him be." Joy-in-the-Dance put a restraining hand on Catch-a-Tick's shoulder. "I'm interested to know what the king of Arkadia's doing here."

"That's a king?" said Catch-a-Tick.

"Never. Not me." Bromios sat down heavily and tossed aside the empty cook pot. "Nothing to do with kings. I'm a humble peasant."

"Your Majesty," said Lucian, "I know you're the king. I've seen you a hundred times in the palace."

"What palace? Don't bedevil me, boy. Where's more food?"

"I was one of your clerks," Lucian insisted.

"He's really the king?" put in Catch-a-Tick. "You're face-to-face with your mortal enemy! Go at him, Aiee-Ouch. Hit him with the cook pot. Smite him down!"

"Keep out of this," Lucian said. "I'm not smiting anybody."

"You're showing mercy." Catch-a-Tick nodded. "That's heroic, too. But not as good as smiting."

"I could try my hand at a little smiting." Oudeis stepped up to Bromios and shook a fist. "You miserable specimen of a monarch, you're at the bottom of everyone's troubles, including mine. What you started ended up with me transporting a talking jackass, losing my ship, nearly drowning—"

"That's right," broke in Fronto, too indignant to keep silent. "It's a chain of circumstances, cause and effect. And when we come to the effect of our being here in deplorable circumstances, you're the cause."

"Cause? Of what?" said Bromios. "I have nothing to do with a jackass."

"A poet, actually," corrected Fronto. "You're to blame for what's happened to all of us."

"Poet?" Bromios squinted at him. "I never met one, but you're not what I might have expected."

"I never met a king," returned Fronto, "and I could say the same."

"And don't blame me for your troubles. They're no fault of mine."

"Whose, then?" said Joy-in-the-Dance.

Bromios groaned. "That monstrous Woman-Who-Talks-to-Snakes. I wish I could lay hands on her."

"What would you do?"

"Do?" cried Bromios. "I know just what I'd do. I—" He stopped as if the wind had suddenly leaked out of him, and put his head in his hands. When he finally looked up, he spoke barely above a whisper: "I'd beg forgiveness."

"You'd what?" exclaimed Joy-in-the-Dance.

"Yes, I'd beg forgiveness. Oh, I admit I vowed revenge. Calchas and Phobos couldn't have been happier. But, since then, nothing's gone right. Planting? Not done as it should be. The harvest? Who knows if there'll even be one. Sickness? No wise-women to cure it. The people are against me, men and women alike, and that's a pain-ful state of affairs. I don't like being hated. A king has feelings, too, you know."

"You should have thought of that before you wrecked everything," said Oudeis.

"I'm not good at thinking," protested Bromios. "Cal-chas and Phobos are supposed to do that sort of thing for me. But I'm not blind. I saw how badly I'd done. The Lady's followers were the only ones who knew how to get us out of the mess. I wanted to take back my decrees.

"Calchas and Phobos wouldn't hear of it. They want-ed to crack down even harder. I couldn't understand that. They knew things were getting worse. But I overheard them, one night, chuckling about what good fortune it was, food and everything else starting to be in short sup-ply. That's a puzzler."

"Not to me," said Lucian. "I think I understand it very well. I kept your palace accounts. I found out that they were cheating you already. I'll make a good guess they're buying up everything they can lay hands on to sell later at ten times the price. Simple as that."

"If you say so," replied Bromios. "Arithmetic's beyond me. All I know is: The more I wanted to take back the decrees, the more they talked against it. When I told them I'd do it no matter what they said, they came out with a better notion.

"A great honor and privilege is what they had in mind for me," Bromios went on. "The grandest, noblest deed a king could do. The chance of a lifetime: the rite of immolation."

"Right of who?" said Catch-a-Tick. "Moles?"

"Not *r-i-g-h-t*," said Fronto, "but *r-i-t-e*. We poets call that a homonym. It sounds the same, but it's different. Immolation—they were going to sacrifice him."

"They made it out to be a wonderful opportunity," said Bromios. "Not every king was so lucky."

"Bromios," Joy-in-the-Dance said, "didn't you understand? They were going to kill you."

"Not permanently," said Bromios. "They explained it very clearly. In the olden days, when things went badly, to set them right again the king gave his life for his people. But—and here's the best part—after he's sacrificed, he goes to the Great Hall of the Sky Bear; feasting, revelry, merrymaking, all he could want. Then he comes back here, good as new. I'd have a star named for me, too. Even a whole constellation."

"You didn't believe them, did you?" said Lucian.

"Well, yes, I did. At first," said Bromios. "But after I thought it over for a couple of days, I didn't much fancy the idea. I'm a warrior, I've seen dead people. They didn't look in any kind of shape to do anything, let alone come back to life. A king, now, maybe that's different. Or maybe not. Even so, I got to wondering: Suppose something goes wrong? Suppose I lose my way to the Great Hall? Or who knows what? Do I just drift around forever? It's an honor having stars named after you, but cold comfort, when you come right down to it. I thanked them for the opportunity but said I'd decided to pass it up.

"They told me it was too late," Bromios continued. "I was already marked down for sacrifice. They set a guard over me, then. To make sure no harm came to me while they got ready for the ceremony. Well, I didn't want any part of it. I knocked a couple of heads together and slipped out of the palace.

"They sent warriors—my own troops!—after me. Once, they nearly caught me. They're still hunting me, like some sort of animal. I've been running ever since, hiding in bushes and burrows, with hardly a wink of sleep, nor bite of food, nor drop to drink."

The king's burly shoulders sagged. "Where can I go? What can I do? If I could only talk to the pythoness again, plead with her to have mercy and save me. But she's gone. I'm lost. I'll be a constellation, like it or not."

"Bromios," Joy-in-the-Dance said quietly, "I'm Woman-Who-Talks-to-Snakes."

"Don't mock me," Bromios moaned. "That's a cruel joke."

"It takes a while to get used to the idea," said Lucian,

"but it's true. She's also the daughter of the Lady of Wild Things."

"No such person," Bromios said. "She doesn't exist."

"My mother would be surprised to hear that. As for my being the pythoness—listen."

She raised an arm to screen her face with the cloak and began, "O Bromios, Bromios, your life-threads are spun—"

"That voice! Those words!" The king's jaw dropped and he clapped his hands to his head. "You? It's you?" As the girl nodded, Bromios gave a cry and threw himself at her feet. "Forgive me! Have mercy!"

"Forgiveness is something you'd have to talk over with my mother," said Joy-in-the-Dance. "Mercy? You're welcome to mine, if it makes you feel better. In a practical sense, it won't much help you."

"Nor will we," put in Oudeis. "Frankly, your pathetic tale doesn't tug at my heart. You've taken our time, eaten our food, and I think you'd best shove off. We're in a hurry. The jackass here has to reach Callista—"

"The island?" Bromios stopped groveling and looked up eagerly. "I'd be safe there. They'd never find me."

"Oudeis," Joy-in-the-Dance began, "talking about practical help, do you suppose we could bring him along—?

"Absolutely not," declared Oudeis. "It's bad enough shipping out with an ass. No runaway kings."

"He's a sorry example of a king, I admit," said Ops. "But he's still a person."

"Noble soul!" cried Bromios, seizing Ops by the hand. "Thank you for those words. What royalty of spirit! I wish I'd had some of it."

"Fronto's the one to decide," put in Lucian. "He's the most concerned. He should say who goes and who doesn't."

"I have to agree with Ops," said Fronto, after some moments. "There's not much king in him, but he is a human being. Which is more than I can say for myself. Yes, take him with us."

"Dearest friend!" Bromios flung his arm around Fronto's neck. "What did you say your name was? Calchas and Phobos never had a good word for poets. Idle, untrustworthy riffraff is what they called them. I see they were wrong about that, too."

✤

If Bromios resembled little of his former self, Oudeis tried to make him even less so. With his knife, the shipmaster hacked at the king's hair and beard, stained his face with berry juice, and set Fronto's straw hat to shadow his brow.

"Best I can do," said Oudeis while Bromios underwent the shipmaster's finishing touches in patient silence.

"There's a lot of him, and I can't change his size. But, if he keeps his trap shut and doesn't call attention to himself, he'll pass well enough for an upcountry lout."

Next morning, they set off again, Bromios striding between Fronto and Ops, his newest and dearest companions. As the king's spirits revived, so did his appetite. The remaining supplies and what Joy-in-the-Dance could gather did nothing to take the edge off it. No sooner had he downed his portion than he looked around, hopefully licking his chops. When Ops thought no one was watching, he handed the king a good share of his own rations. As it turned out, so did Lucian and everyone else.

For the most part, Bromios was pathetically grateful and anxious to be helpful. From time to time, however, he forgot he was a runaway sacrifice. Each time his thoughts turned to Calchas and Phobos, he growled and muttered, threatened awful punishments, kicked tree trunks, and snapped branches as if they were the soothsayers' necks. After offering to tend the fire, he usually let it go out; or neglected to clean the pot, as Oudeis ordered; or made messes, which he regally ignored.

"It's rather like having a tame bear for a pet," Fronto observed. "You can't help being fond of him, but you keep wishing he were a cat."

No one, however, not even Oudeis, suggested abandoning him. The shipmaster, at first, had feared that

Bromios would hinder them. On the contrary, the royal sacrifice set such a pace that they reached the outskirts of Metara two days sooner than Oudeis reckoned. As he promised, Oudeis did not venture into the city. Instead, he turned off and took a roundabout way seaward, following the narrow beach in the shadow of high cliffs. Not long after midday, the harbor opened in front of them.

"The port—just as you told me, Aiee-Ouch!" Catch-a-Tick stared, round-eyed. "The boats—herds of them! And people—I've never seen so many all at once!"

There were, in fact, fewer passersby than Lucian expected. Among the vessels at the landing stages, only one was being offloaded, and none taking on cargo. Many shops stood empty; the stalls of fishmongers and vegetable sellers displayed hardly any wares. Oudeis stopped in front of the first tavern they came to and motioned them to go in.

"Wait for me there," the shipmaster ordered. "I'll be back in no time, with money in my purse and quick passage out. No, not you," he told Fronto, who had started for the tavern. "Stand outside. You're still an ass, so behave like a proper one."

"I'll stay with him," Lucian said as Oudeis hurried down to the waterfront and the others led Bromios through the tavern door.

Fronto had trotted a little way along the street, where he gazed anxiously seaward. "I pray Earth-Shaker gives us a speedy voyage. We'll reach Callista none too soon. Haw! Haw! There—haw!—it goes again. Dear boy, I'm more donkey than ever."

"You're tired, overexcited." Lucian put as much assurance as possible into words he did not entirely believe. He was much aware that Fronto had been snorting and braying more than usual.

"Trust Oudeis," he said, patting Fronto's neck. "If he promised to get you there—"

"Thief!" roared a voice in Lucian's ear.

A heavy hand gripped him by the scruff of the neck. Shaken and buffeted, Lucian was roughly spun around to find himself nose to nose with Cerdo.

24

The Hall of Sacrifice

The donkey robber!" Cerdo shook him until his teeth rattled. "Got you! I'll teach you to steal my beast."

Lucian scuffled free of the merchant's grip. "Not yours! He's mine!"

"Liar! There's my brand on his rump. I'll have him back, and I'll have your hide into the bargain!"

Fronto, horrified to recognize his brutal master, bucked and reared, braying at the top of his lungs. Seeing the enraged merchant start after Lucian again, the poet laid back his ears and snapped his jaws, nipping whatever parts of Cerdo he could reach.

"Help! Help!" bawled the merchant as Fronto's attack from behind rousted him off his feet. "Save me! It's a killer jackass!"

A handful of waterfront idlers had already gathered; passersby, sniffing possible amusement, hurried to watch as Cerdo, scrambling up, seized Fronto's tail while Lucian clung to his neck, and both hauled in opposite directions. The commotion had also caught the attention of a mounted patrol of warriors, who plunged their horses through the crowd.

"Arrest him!" Cerdo stabbed an accusing finger at Lucian. "He stole my property. This ass is from my pack train. There's the rest of them, down there." He waved toward the dock where goods were being unloaded. "You look at the brand on him. And this young villain—he's a runaway from the palace."

"I'm a soldier, not a judge. This is a case for a magistrate—Here, now, just hold on a minute." The captain had been eyeing Lucian. "I've seen this fellow before."

"Not me," blurted Lucian. "I'm somebody else."

"I commandeered his donkey as royal property, then it got stolen from me. This is a murky business," the officer added. "Until it's settled, I'm impounding the ass. You, too, my fine fellow. You'll both come along with me."

"By thunder, no, they won't!"

Bromios had shouldered his way past the onlookers, with Joy-in-the-Dance tugging at his cloak and Ops doing his best to hold him back.

"What's one of my troop captains doing in a wrangle over a jackass?" Bromios put his hands on his hips and thrust out his jaw. "Back off. Get about your duties. Let him be, he's my friend. The lad, too. They all are," he went on while Joy-in-the-Dance kept signaling him to hold his tongue.

The officer squinted and rubbed his eyes. "Your Majesty?"

"Who else?" shouted Bromios. "Are you deaf as well as blind? I gave you an order. Do it, blast you! I'm your king."

The onlookers gasped and drew back. The officer hesitated, shifting uneasily on his mount. "Your Majesty —in this case, your soothsayers are authorities even higher than you. Their command—if you're found, you're to be escorted to the palace."

"Nobody's escorting anybody anywhere," said Joy-in-the-Dance.

"Don't try anything," whispered Lucian. "They'll find out who you are."

The captain had drawn his sword. Bromios strode up to him. "You dare threaten me?"

"Not you, Majesty," said the officer. "You're the royal sacrifice. Your person is sacred. Forgive me, but I have to take you in. If your friends hinder me, I'll have my men cut them down. You come quietly, Majesty, and they go free."

Bromios glared and chewed his lips. At last, he nodded. "So be it." His face wrinkled as he turned to embrace Joy-in-the-Dance, Lucian, and Ops, and he patted Catch-a-Tick on the head. He laid a stubbly cheek on Fronto's nose. "A swift and happy voyage, friend. You did your best for me, all of you.

"Eh, eh, no glooming," he added. "I'll be back good as new. You'll see some changes, then, starting with Calchas and Phobos. If not—well, you look for my star. I'll wink at you, so you'll know it's me."

"My property!" squealed Cerdo as the king swung up behind the captain.

"Find a magistrate." The officer waved him aside. "I've got more important business."

The patrol closed around Bromios and galloped off. Helpless to stop them, Lucian turned to face a closer, louder threat: Cerdo, bawling for watchmen and constables.

"Get him off the street," Lucian ordered, "before he stirs up the whole port."

Between them, Lucian and Ops hauled the sputtering merchant into the tavern and flung him down on a stool.

"I'll deal with this," said Joy-in-the-Dance. "Listen to

me, Cerdo. One peep and I'll do something you won't like."

"Thieves! Villains!" yelled Cerdo. "I'll have the law on all of you."

"Don't say I didn't warn you." Joy-in-the-Dance made quick gestures at the merchant. "Here, look. How awful! See—Oh, this is dreadful! Your beard's on fire. The flames! They're going up your nose."

Cerdo screamed and beat his face with his hands.

"It's all right now. The fire's out. That really must have smarted," said Joy-in-the-Dance. "But you're going to keep your mouth shut, aren't you?" The terrified merchant nodded. "Good. Make sure you do."

Fronto, meantime, had trotted into the tavern. At the sight of a donkey in her establishment, the proprietress snatched up a broom. "No donkeys here! Out, out, shoo!"

That same instant, Oudeis burst through the door. "What's amiss? There's talk that Bromios was taken—" He stopped short and stared at the tavern mistress. "My honey-girl? Mirina?"

The stout, gray-haired woman dropped the broom and stared back. "Oudeis?" With a joyous outcry, she ran to fling her arms around him. "Where have you been? I've waited and waited for you all these years. This is my tavern. My uncle left me money to buy it. I've kept it for us. I'd almost lost hope—"

"Dearest Mirina, more beautiful than ever," exclaimed Oudeis, wiping a tear from his eye. "How I've longed for you. But, my sweet, when last we met I recall you threw a pot at my head, tossed crockery at me, laid into me with a broom—"

"Numbskull!" retorted Mirina. "It didn't mean I wanted you to go away."

"No matter, I'm home to stay," said Oudeis. "Almost." He turned to Fronto. "I have a ship. We sail for Callista on the morning tide."

"What?" Mirina picked up the broom and shook it at Oudeis. "Sail where? You wretch, I've turned down a dozen offers of marriage for your sake. Don't you talk to me about sailing."

"Please, please, my little darling, I'll explain it later." Oudeis turned back to Fronto. "You're in luck. It's the only vessel I could get. Nothing else for weeks. It's your best chance; and, I daresay, your last.

"Sweet one," Oudeis added, "bar the door. No intruders. Now, quick, what's this about Bromios?"

"Don't be alarmed to hear me speak," Fronto whispered to Mirina. "You see, something quite astonishing happened."

"With that here-today-gone-tomorrow Oudeis home when I'd about given him up for dead," replied Mirina, "nothing astonishes me, least of all a talking jackass."

"Oudeis, it's true," Lucian said. "Bromios ran out to help Fronto and me. A patrol recognized him. He gave himself up so they wouldn't arrest us. Cerdo, that scoundrel sitting there, set off the whole thing."

"I'm truly sorry." Oudeis sadly shook his head. "I'd grown fond of the lout. At the last, he did you a good turn. For us, now: We go aboard after nightfall—"

"They're going to kill Bromios," Lucian broke in. "Don't you understand? We can't let them."

"Lad, that's out of our hands," replied Oudeis.

"Not if I can help it," put in Joy-in-the-Dance. "There has to be a way to save him. If we can get to him—"

"What?" cried Oudeis. "Have you lost your wits? You, the pythoness? They'll kill you along with Bromios. And you, too," he added to Lucian. "And you, jackass, you can't risk a delay. And there you have three good reasons not to set foot in the palace even if you could."

"And one best reason why we have to," said Joy-in-the-Dance. "Listen to me, Oudeis. If Bromios is sacrificed, who rules Arkadia? Calchas and Phobos, of course. They'll claim they're just looking after things until Bromios comes back. Which he won't. Meantime, you'll have disaster worse than ever.

"But if we rescue him," she went on, "he'll have learned a good lesson. He'll have sense enough to get rid of that pair. He said he wanted to take back all his decrees. He can't do that if he's dead, can he?"

"I'm not a statesman," said Oudeis. "That's no business of mine."

"Oh, yes it is." Mirina shook the broom at him. "I've heard of new laws in store that won't let women own so much as a stick of property. And there goes my tavern. You want to sail to Callista? All right, I'll wait for you again. But if you won't help this young lady, who seems a lot cleverer than you, I'll do more than throw a pot at you."

"There's still another best reason," put in Fronto. "Bromios called us his friends. Poor fellow, at this point we're the only friends he has."

"Stop, enough!" cried Oudeis. "Yes, I admit it goes against my grain to do nothing for the poor lubber. But what? You tell me that and I'm with you."

"To begin with, we have to get inside the palace," Lucian said. "I know how to do it."

"Of course you do," said Catch-a-Tick.

"Cerdo's a royal purveyor," Lucian went on. "He's in and out all the time. He'll take us along with his pack train. No one will question him."

"Aiee-Ouch," said Joy-in-the-Dance, "for once you have an interesting idea."

Cerdo opened his mouth to protest but closed it rapidly at a look from Joy-in-the-Dance.

"You will do exactly as you're told," she said. "Otherwise, you'll have more than your beard on fire."

"There's a stableman," Lucian continued. "Menyas, an old friend of mine. He'll help us if anyone can."

"Aye, lad, I'll give you credit," Oudeis admitted, after a moment. "You could be on to something that might work. So far, so good. Now, let's say we get ourselves into the palace. What next?"

"After that," said Lucian, "what we do is—yes, well, what we do is"—he paused and shook his head—"I haven't the least idea."

"Oh, a marvelous plan," retorted Oudeis, rolling his eyes.

"Better than nothing," said Joy-in-the-Dance. "We'll do it."

"We will?" said Lucian.

⬙

With Ops on one side of Cerdo and Joy-in-the-Dance on the other to prod the merchant along, they left the tavern and hurried down the waterfront. Mirina had insisted on joining them to keep an eye on Oudeis. "I've waited this long for the footloose rogue, I'm not letting him out of my sight."

The merchant's pack animals were already laden with bales and baskets. Tethered one behind the other, a couple of mules, a swaybacked horse, and eight or nine scrawny donkeys waited in gloomy resignation.

"I see some of my companions in misery," Fronto murmured. "Yes, there's poor old Lop-Ear. And Spindleshanks. Ah, my boy, I shudder to think I used to be one of them."

"I'm afraid you'll have to be one of them again," said Lucian. "Just a little while."

"A little while may be all I—haw—have," replied Fronto. "Running into that vile Cerdo again seems to have frightened more speech out of me."

As Lucian instructed, Fronto took his place at the head of the train. Joy-in-the-Dance whispered to Cerdo: "Tell your people you've hired extra hands for this delivery. That's all. Not a peep more. Don't even blink."

Protectively clutching his beard, Cerdo obeyed the girl's orders. Far from being suspicious, his servants appeared glad for the added help. The pack train, with Fronto leading, set off as quickly as their burdens allowed. Catch-a-Tick skipped at the rear, urging stragglers to keep pace.

A little after sundown, they reached the back gate of the palace. So accustomed to the arrival of the merchant and his goods, the sentry waved him and his animals into the yard, only remarking that he was later than usual.

Lucian halted near the storehouses. A chill ran through him. Never had he imagined setting foot in this place again; and he still had no idea what next to do. Ops and Joy-in-the-Dance had started unburdening the animals. Lucian looked around for Menyas.

He saw nothing of him in the stables, then sighted him by one of the granaries. The old stableman's face was gray and careworn, and he seemed older than Lucian remembered.

Lucian ran to him. Menyas blinked, hardly recognizing him, then gave a glad cry. "Lad, is that yourself? Here?" He glanced about hastily. "Get into the stable. It's worth your neck if you're caught—"

"Never mind that. My friends are with me. We want Bromios." Lucian drew him aside. "The sacrifice—we have to stop it."

"Are you out of your head? First, why meddle in such a business? Second, there's naught you can do."

"There must be." As quickly as he could, Lucian stammered out what had happened since meeting Bromios. "Where's the king now?"

"Lad, I don't make sense of half what you're babbling. The king? He's to be offered up when the Bear Star rises." Menyas squinted at the darkening sky. "Any time now.

You won't save him. They've already got him in the Hall of Sacrifice."

Without waiting to hear more, leaving Menyas standing bewildered, Lucian shouted for Joy-in-the-Dance and Ops. The girl threw aside the basket she was unloading and started after him. Cerdo, seizing the chance to escape, bawled for help at the top of his voice and scurried across the yard, Ops at his heels. The pack animals brayed and whinnied, straining at their tethers. From the tail of his eye, Lucian glimpsed guards racing to the stables.

Not daring a backward glance, he dashed down the walkways, past the sheds and chicken run. Footsteps clattered from behind him, and then Catch-a-Tick was racing at his side.

"Aiee-Ouch, I want to see you do the rest of your plan," he called out. "I want to be there when it happens."

"Stay out of this. Go back. Fetch the pythoness. And Ops."

"They're busy. You see, what happened—"

"Then go help."

Catch-a-Tick paid no attention to him. Wasting no more time or breath trying to shake him off, Lucian pressed on. Torches lined the pathway to the Hall of Sacrifice. Two warriors guarded the open portals. Skirting the hall, Lucian cast around for another entry. The lath and plaster building was open-sided, with rows of wooden pillars holding up the roof. Calchas and Phobos ordinarily used it for consulting the oracular chickens. Now it was filled with palace officials come to witness the solemn ceremony. A low wall of boards ran between the pillars. Lucian scrambled to the top of it. Catch-a-Tick climbed up beside him.

"What next, Aiee-Ouch?"

Lucian did not answer. His eyes had gone to the far end of the hall. Crimson draperies hung from the rafters overhead. Tall iron braziers flamed on both sides of the stone altar where Bromios, in a drugged stupor, lay in his bearskin regalia. Calchas held a long, glittering knife. Phobos was gazing beyond the pillars into the night sky. For some long moments he stood watching, then turned and nodded. "The Bear Star has risen." Calchas lifted the blade high above his head.

The throng held its breath. Lucian, frozen, could only stare as Catch-a-Tick nudged him anxiously. Then he burst out with the only words that sprang to his lips.

"No! Stop!"

Calchas hesitated and glared around. "Who dares to speak?"

"The sacrifice is not acceptable," cried Lucian. "These

soothsayers are unworthy to perform it. Their hearts are stained with crime. Thieves and traitors!"

"The tongue of a liar!" Calchas had fixed a furious eye on Lucian, who was standing on the wall. The crowd murmured uneasily. "Seize him. Fetch him here."

Phobos was frantically gesturing for Calchas to strike. "Do it, you fool. Do it."

Lucian's heart sank. The crowd was too thick for him to force his way through and make one desperate attempt to seize the blade from Calchas. Then it flashed into his mind: the gift from Catch-a-Tick. The sling.

He snatched the bag from his tunic, fumbled a stone into the pouch, and whirled the thongs around his head. The missile whirred through the air.

It missed its mark.

He had taken dead aim at Calchas. To his horror, that same instant, Bromios sat up. The stone struck the king squarely on the head. Bromios toppled off the slab.

Catch-a-Tick crowed triumphantly. "You saved him! Marvelous!"

It took a moment for Lucian to understand. The stone had knocked Bromios to the ground just as Calchas brought down the knife. The blade shattered on the empty altar.

Lucian sprang from the wall. Bromios, dazed, stumbled to his feet and lurched into a smoking brazier. The red-hot coals went flying, the crimson draperies burst into flame. Phobos, yelping as sparks showered him, streaked for the open side of the hall.

But Calchas would not be cheated of his victim. Even as the flames licked at the rafters, he snatched up a cleaver from behind the altar and swung it wildly at the reeling Bromios. By then, Lucian was upon him. The soothsayer turned to face his attacker.

"Watch out for that cleaver, Aiee-Ouch!" cried Catch-a-Tick.

Calchas halted in midstroke. Cerdo had dashed into the hall. As the onlookers scattered, the merchant streaked toward Calchas, bawling for help. Behind him, braying and snapping, galloped Fronto and all of Cerdo's donkeys.

Making straight for Calchas, Fronto reared and lashed out with his hooves. Calchas jumped back and flung away the cleaver. The roof had begun blazing like matchwood. A burning rafter fell in a fountain of sparks, striking Bromios across the shoulders and sending him headlong to the ground.

The onlookers, shouting in panic, jostled their way out of the hall. Cerdo dived over the wall. The pursuing donkeys jumped after him. The fire, by now, had spread to the nearby sheds and outbuildings. Catch-a-Tick was dancing with gleeful excitement.

"Aiee-Ouch, you're burning down the whole palace!"

"Get out!" Lucian struggled to lift the king to Fronto's back. The blazing rafters collapsed. The roof fell in on itself. Lucian gave an anguished cry. Fronto lay beneath the crackling timber. Lucian plunged into the flames.

"No use," Fronto gasped. "Save yourself, my boy. Too late for Callista. I can barely speak. Leave me here. Better a dead poet than a live jackass."

Lucian flung up his arms as a curtain of fire swept over Fronto. Choking, blinded by smoke, Lucian groped helplessly. Fronto had vanished.

Strong hands gripped Lucian's shoulders and dragged him clear of the burning wreckage. He tried to fight free of his rescuers. Joy-in-the-Dance was there; beside her were Buckthorn and See-Far-Ahead.

25

A City in Ashes

Nothing was spared. The fire had raged all night, sweeping over sheds and storehouses. Half the palace had been gutted; the rest was smoke-blackened or gnawed by flames. Clouds of ash sifted down on the rooftops, turning the city gray. About dawn, a sour little rain began, the droplets hissing and steaming as they touched the hot embers. Menyas and some household servants had gotten the horses and livestock to safety. Of the palace officials, most had fled; only a handful of warriors stayed at their posts. Some fifty of the Horse Clan who had ridden with See-Far-Ahead kept as much order as possible among the city dwellers. The folk of Metara had never seen the like of these tall, graceful men and women, and stared with wonder at them, as if they were beings from an unknown, marvelous world.

"The Lady of Wild Things had news from the eagle that followed you," See-Far-Ahead later told Lucian. "When Bromios came upon you, she feared for your lives. Though she could not be sure of its nature, she sensed that great peril lay ahead. She urged me to summon warriors and ride with all speed for Metara while she herself made ready to set sail and join us here.

"As we passed through the domain of the Goat Folk, Buckthorn asked to accompany us. There was the matter of a certain disobedient young member of his family," See-Far-Ahead went on. "Only the wind itself could have gone more swiftly than we did. Alas, we came too late. Now my heart aches for your friend and for you."

In the morning, when it was barely light enough to see, with Bromios in the care of Ops and Mirina, Lucian and the others picked their way through the rubble to what had been the Hall of Sacrifice. Joy-in-the-Dance kept his hand clasped in hers. Since Lucian had been pulled from the wreckage, the two had never been out of each other's sight, and rarely out of each other's touch.

The Hall of Sacrifice had burned to the ground. The heaviest rafters still smoldered; the reek of charred wood caught in Lucian's throat; his eyes watered in the haze of smoke. Or so he thought, until he realized he was weeping. See-Far-Ahead and Buckthorn set about heaving aside what remained of the fallen timbers.

"There's naught here, lad," Buckthorn said gently. "All burned beyond a trace. Let be," he added as Lucian searched through the wreckage. "Take no more grief than you can bear."

Catch-a-Tick's face puckered and he leaned his cheek on Lucian's arm as Joy-in-the-Dance led them back to the stable yard. Menyas had found some sheets of canvas and Oudeis began rigging a makeshift awning to keep out most of the rain. Bromios, still in what remained of his bearskin cloak, was sitting up. The drug had worn off and he looked not much the worse for being nearly sacrificed.

"Any sign of our friend?" The king's face fell as Lucian shook his head. "No, I was afraid not. I'm sorry. He'd be on his way to Callista by now if it hadn't been for me. The rest of the prophecy's come true, the city's in ashes; but I didn't think it would cost his life instead of mine."

"I wonder if there's a constellation for jackasses," added Bromios. "If there is, he deserves to have one." He turned to Lucian. "As for constellations, thanks to you I'm not one of them. You saved my hide with that business about an unacceptable sacrifice. I never heard of such a rule."

"Neither did I," said Lucian.

"It was all part of his plan," put in Catch-a-Tick. "Just like hitting you instead of the fat fellow. Who but Aiee-Ouch would have thought of doing it? Or setting loose the donkeys?"

"Listen to me," said Lucian, "none of it was any plan of mine."

"The donkeys were Fronto's idea," said Joy-in-the-Dance. "He was afraid his time was short, he wanted a chance for himself and the others to get some of their own back on Cerdo." She smiled at the recollection. "Fronto called it 'jackass liberation.' What he most wanted, though, was to help Aiee-Ouch."

"He did," said Lucian. "In the nick of time, just as if it had been a tale. Hitting Bromios by mistake—he'd have thought that was a nice touch.

"He did more than save my life," Lucian went on. "He gave me a new one. He told me I should be a storyteller—that I was a storyteller already and didn't know it. I've been turning it over and over in my mind. I'm not sure he was right, but that's what I'll try to be."

"I know he was right," said Joy-in-the-Dance, adding fondly, "do you remember that preposterous tale you told me when we first met? As truth, it was ridiculous. As a story—it wasn't all that bad. You'll learn to do better. If Fronto set you on your occupation, he gave you a great gift."

"I'll find out soon enough if it's true," Lucian said, brightening. "He told me he'd be pleased and proud if I were his colleague. I only wish he knew."

"Perhaps he does," put in Bromios. "I hope so, anyway. But, speaking of gifts, you tell me what I can do for you."

"There's nothing." Lucian shook his head. "I'd only ask you to be a better king."

"No," declared Bromios. "Certainly not. I won't be a better king. I can't," he pressed on despite an indignant outcry from Joy-in-the-Dance. "Because I'm not a king at all. You have a new one. As royal a fellow as ever you'll find. King Ops."

"What's he saying?" exclaimed Lucian, turning to the scapegoat. "Is that true? You're the king of Arkadia?"

"I'm afraid so," admitted Ops. "At first, I told him it was out of the question, but he kept at me. He was very persuasive. He vowed he'd crack my head if I didn't accept."

"That's wonderful!" Lucian clasped the former scapegoat's hand. "Congratulations—Your Majesty!"

"Ops, that's the only wise thing Bromios has ever done," said Joy-in-the-Dance, embracing him. "It makes perfect sense. Your father was of the Bear tribe; your mother, of our people. You're both. If anyone can settle our differences, you can."

"You'll still have your old occupation," added Lucian. "You like taking on people's troubles. Now, you'll have a whole kingdom to serve."

"I hadn't looked at it that way," said Ops. "Yes, it does save wandering about. And I'll set up councils with both men and women."

He stopped as a disheveled figure edged his way into the shelter. The intruder's face was smudged with ashes, his lank hair tangled and matted; his only garment, a length of tattered cloth, with holes burnt in it, which he had wrapped around himself as best he could.

"Here, now, what are you after?" demanded Oudeis. "We're having a serious, private conversation."

"We just got a new king," piped up Catch-a-Tick. "He's King Ops."

"Really?" said the new arrival. "Marvelous news! I'm delighted to hear it. Let me be the first to wish him well, if the rest of you haven't done it already."

From the moment he had begun to speak, Joy-in-the-Dance had fixed her glance on him, studying him intently. Lucian, too, had been watching and listening, all the more bewildered as the stranger, smiling happily, continued.

"It will be my great joy, honor, and privilege to write a coronation ode—"

Lucian jumped to his feet, staring speechless. His ears were playing tricks on him. He dared not believe what they were telling him.

"Dear boy, I'm not a ghost. If I were, I'd hope to be a little less famished."

"Fronto?" Lucian gasped. "You're not. You can't be."

"Can be. And am," replied the poet as Joy-in-the-Dance drew closer, her eyes lighting up. "Yes, beyond question, I'm me. Myself again, altogether in splendid shape—my usual shape, that is. I have a tender spot where Cerdo put his mark on me, but I expect it will fade away in time.

"I hope I didn't cause undue concern," Fronto went on. "I got here as quickly as I could. I do admit I wasn't sure, at first, if I'd get here at all."

"But you were burned up," Lucian stammered. "I know—I saw—"

"Aiee-Ouch, be quiet," said Joy-in-the-Dance. "Let him tell us."

"Yes, well," said Fronto, "if you recall, the Lady of Wild Things mentioned using a blazing pyre to transform me. She didn't recommend it, and I quite understand why. Indeed, I might have been burned to a crisp. In fact, I was. So to speak. My jackass exterior, in any case. Of that, there was nothing left at all.

"Of myself—I can't describe it precisely, I was neither

here nor there, neither one place nor the other. Betwixt and between, you might say. For a while, I had the impression I was turning into a tree. Then a bird. Then a fish, a rabbit, a hedgehog, and half a dozen other creatures one after the other.

"Until my own body came back, I had no idea who was who or which way was which. An unsettling condition, but a very interesting one, as I look back on it. For us poets, a state of confusion is quite ordinary.

"When I did, at last, come to myself, I still had one trivial difficulty. My clothes had vanished along with my hooves, tail, and the rest. I could hardly, out of modesty, go parading around like that. These bits and pieces were all I found, but they'll do for the moment.

"And so, I'm overjoyed to be with you all—Haw! Haw! Ah—don't worry about the occasional hee-haw. Old habits tend to linger."

"Fronto," said Lucian, embracing him, "it's you. It really is."

"Was there ever any doubt?" said Fronto.

26

New Metara

The Lady of Wild Things was in Metara. Watchers at the port had, from a distance, sighted the golden sail and banks of flashing oars; and, by the time the long, slender vessel glided into the harbor, word had spread from one end of the city to the other. See-Far-Ahead and his horsemen galloped to escort her from the landing stage. If the townsfolk had marveled at these splendid riders, they stood speechless in even greater wonder as the procession made its way to the public square. The jeweled diadem shining at her brow, a blue sea-cloak around her shoulders, her leopards padding beside her, the Lady of Wild Things moved with graceful strides at the head of her white-robed Daughters of Morning.

At first, the crowds lining the streets hardly dared

whisper among themselves. Some had never believed that she existed; those who did believe had never dreamed she would set foot in Metara and they would see her with their own eyes. Then, one voice rose, another, and another until it seemed the whole city had joined in a single joyous outcry.

As the Lady of Wild Things entered the stable yard, Joy-in-the-Dance ran to her arms. Lucian felt his heart clench as the Lady's last words to him came back as piercingly as when she had spoken them: *That is her life. You can have no part in it.*

"Lord See-Far-Ahead has told me all that has happened," the Lady of Wild Things said. "I am indebted to him for his help, though I understand it was little needed." Before she could say more, Fronto, unable to restrain himself, eagerly hurried forward.

"Dear Lady, I'm myself again," he began, bowing deeply. "In case you don't recognize me—"

"Poet," the Lady said, "I would recognize you anywhere, jackass or otherwise. I am happy to see you in your own form. That much is settled, but other questions remain."

"Yes, and one of them has to do with me," put in Bromios, who had been shifting uneasily back and forth. He ventured to approach and then knelt at the Lady's feet. "The pythoness showed me more mercy than I deserve. I don't expect forgiveness, but I'll beg it from you anyway."

"King who used to be," replied the Lady, "as I forgave this poet for being an ass, so I forgive you for being a fool. You played your part, however unwittingly, in fulfilling the prophecy."

"Oh, it worked out," Bromios ruefully answered, "exactly as the pythoness foretold."

"But not as you understood it." The Lady of Wild Things turned to Ops. "*Khaire*, Argeus Bright-Face. The prophecy spoke of a king in rags. It was you, not Bromios."

"Dear Bright-Face! What have they gone and done to you?" Laurel-Crown broke away from the other Daughters of Morning to fling her arms around him. "Lay a burden like that on you?"

"I really hadn't much to say about it," said Ops, beaming at her. "I wanted an occupation and that's what it turned out to be. I hope you don't object."

"We'll have to make the best of it," said Laurel-Crown. "I had other things in mind for us, but we'll manage—"

"Return to your place," the Lady ordered. "I have more urgent matters to settle: my daughter and this Lucian Aiee-Ouch."

"Punish me any way you choose." Joy-in-the-Dance

stepped to Lucian's side. "We won't be kept apart."

"Be not too severe, Amaranth Flower-Never-Fading." See-Far-Ahead laid a hand on the Lady's arm. "Think of a young warrior and a certain sanctuary maiden. Against her mother's wishes, did she not ride by night to his camp, where they exchanged marriage vows? Do you remember?"

"I remember well," said the Lady, giving him a smile overflowing with love. "It is not a question of punishment, but of pardon. Not to grant, but to ask it." Her eyes went to Lucian. "And so, Lucian Aiee-Ouch, I ask your pardon."

So taken aback by her words, Lucian was at first convinced he had misunderstood them. Braced for some terrible judgment, he realized his ears had not deceived him only when the Lady had gone on.

"You have been much in my thoughts since last we met. I saw you then only as my enemy, as I believed all Bear tribe men to be. My eyes were blinded by concern for my child. I did not see you as yourself and as you truly were. You spoke a hard truth when you had courage to tell me that, by judging every Bear man alike, I was scarcely different from Bromios. I know what has befallen you, and that your love for my daughter has never faltered.

"She, too, wished friendship between our peoples.

That, now, is my wish; and so it shall be. Yes, she disobeyed me. But her disobedience also showed me the strength of love in her own heart. Punishment? No. You both have my blessing."

"Do you mean—are you telling us—?" stammered Lucian, all the more bewildered as Joy-in-the-Dance clasped his hand.

"Don't babble," she whispered to him. "Think it over. Even an Aiee-Ouch can figure out what she means."

"Here's one who won't get off as happily," declared Buckthorn, tightening his grip on Catch-a-Tick's ear. "Disobedience and running away? I have something to say to you, and I'll say it with the flat of my hand."

"I only wanted to see Aiee-Ouch being a hero," protested Catch-a-Tick. "Now I want to see him get married."

Oudeis, cocking an eye at the rain clouds, urged all to take shelter under his awning. Mirina offered to lodge everyone in the tavern, including the leopards. "There's room enough," she said, "if some of you squeeze together."

"It is not necessary," said the Lady of Wild Things, allowing Oudeis to lead her, and the others, out of the downpour. "I shall not long remain here. But until the king of Arkadia has a better roof over his head, he and his companions are welcome to the hospitality of my ship."

"Give me a day and a few willing hands," said Oudeis, "and I'll put together something neat and snug here for everybody. It will do nicely while I deal with the rest of the palace. I'll plan out a whole new one," he went on, his enthusiasm growing. "Aye, and see it's built as it should be. For that, of course, I'll need a bit more time, and all the carpenters, all the lumber I can get—"

"Oudeis," Lucian broke in, "you're talking about building in wood. Can you build in—marble?"

"Stupid question. I can build with anything."

"Laurel-Crown told us the finest marble comes from the cliffs near Metara. If you could find quarrymen, stonemasons, devise machines to hoist the slabs—"

"Why, lad, that's finally a task to match my skill." Oudeis pursed his lips and a gleam came into his eyes. "Yes, by thunder, so I'll do."

"If you want a quarry master," said Bromios, "that's work more to my liking than being king ever was. And if Calchas and Phobos, and Cerdo, too, are ever caught, I'll set them to breaking rocks for the rest of their days."

"Done!" cried Oudeis. "I'll begin with the palace, but I won't stop there. I can rebuild the whole city, a new Metara. What a dream!"

"Yes, and while you're dreaming up your grand schemes," Mirina said under her breath, "you'll leave me the hard work of running the tavern. Well, play with your building blocks. It's better than having you go off sailing whenever the mood strikes."

"And in the middle of the public square," Oudeis pressed on, "I can see it now. A monument to the Lady! Columns, porticos—"

The Lady of Wild Things raised her hand. "No city could have a finer architect than you, Clever Oudeis, but I wish no empty monument."

"Why empty?" Lucian asked. "Long ago, your great sanctuary was filled with books of lore and learning. These were destroyed, but they can be written down again and put in the new building."

"Written?" The Lady frowned. "No, that is not our way."

"It used to be, once," said Lucian. "Why not now? Yes, writings can be stolen, or changed, or used for evil purposes. But isn't the risk worth taking? The more people who share knowledge, the greater safeguard for it. Isn't there more danger in ignorance than knowledge?"

The Lady did not reply. Lucian quickly went on.

"It can be a place for teaching, too. Whoever wanted

to could come and learn the arts of healing, the secrets of planting, and all such. Oudeis himself could teach architecture, navigation—"

"I'll be delighted to instruct in poetry," Fronto put in. "After I've learned a little something about it myself."

"So be it," said the Lady, after a long moment. "This house of teaching shall be in my daughter's charge. The cave and pool at Mount Lerna cannot be restored. She can best serve here in Metara, along with any Daughters of Morning who wish to remain."

"You'd do well to attend and study a few things yourself, my boy," Fronto said to Lucian. "A little knowledge never harmed a storyteller."

"I'll do that gladly," said Lucian. "Then," he said to the Lady, "all the tales I've heard from Oudeis, Gold-Horse, Buckthorn—someday I want to write them down so they won't be forgotten. Those and everything that's happened to me, as well. Sometimes," he added, "they all get mixed up together in my head, as if the tales were my life and my life was a tale."

"When you asked what shape your life should take, I could not tell you," the Lady said. "I gather you have learned that for yourself."

"Thanks to Fronto," replied Lucian. "I've already told

him what I want to do. He wasn't surprised. He said I was a storyteller without knowing it."

"Indeed so, my dear colleague," said Fronto. "And, should you need assistance in the way of improving, refurbishing, adding a few nice touches here and there, I'll be happy to instruct you."

"I'll go to school with Aiee-Ouch," declared Catch-a-Tick.

"Oh, no you won't," said Buckthorn. "You'll come along—" He stopped and scratched his jaw. "And yet, from what I've heard of your doings in the wide world, goat herding may have turned too narrow for you. I'll have a bushel of explaining to do to your mother—but, yes, you little goat-scut, stay awhile among your friends. You might learn something besides mischief."

"Settled, then. I'll start my work," said Oudeis. "But, Lady, I seek one favor. If you'd perform a marriage ceremony for Mirina and me, as I promised her years ago?"

"So I shall, Clever Oudeis," said the Lady. "But mind you also help her with the pots and pans while you dream of a new Metara."

During this, Laurel-Crown and Ops, heads together, had been whispering to each other. "My dear Laurel-Crown has chosen to stay here," said Ops, beaming.

"We'd be honored if you'd do the same service for us. I realize this comes rather suddenly—"

"Not to me it doesn't," said Laurel-Crown. "I had it in mind from the moment I set eyes on you."

"Remarkable!" said Ops. "So did I."

"And us?" Lucian said to Joy-in-the-Dance. "If I understood what your mother told me—"

"Yes, Aiee-Ouch," said Joy-in-the-Dance. "I think you finally figured it out."

"What a tale all this would make!" exclaimed Fronto. "My boy, be sure to write it down. As for me, I feel the urge to compose a wedding anthem. I do believe the old inspiration's bubbling up again."

"Poet, my heart is glad for you," said the Lady of Wild Things, beckoning to him. "I could not give what you sought in the pool at Mount Lerna. But," she added, gently kissing Fronto's brow, "I give you my grace and my blessing."

The rain had stopped. A bright band of colors arched across the sky.

So ends our tale, more happily than it began. What remains to tell is that three weddings were celebrated, with singing and dancing throughout Metara. When the Lady of

Wild Things departed, all the city came to watch. At the same time, flights of birds soared overhead, cranes and sandpipers danced on the shore, otters frolicked in the shoals while seals clambered to the rocks and clapped their flippers, and dolphins leaped from the waves. As the ship sailed from the harbor, the Daughters of Morning began a song of farewell, and the melody hung shimmering in the air long afterward.